THE COTTAGE ACROSS THE LAKE

PAUL CARBERRY

Published in Canada by Engen Books, Chapel Arm, NL.

A CIP catalogue record for this book is available from Library and Archives Canada.

ISBN-13: 978-1-77478-103-6

This book is a work of fiction. Names, characters, places and incidents are products of the author's imagination or are used fictitiously. Any resemblance to actual events or locales or persons living or dead is entirely coincidental.

Distributed by:
Engen Books
www.engenbooks.com
submissions@engenbooks.com

First mass market paperback printing: July 2022

Cover Design: Ellen Curtis

THE COTTAGE ACROSS THE LAKE

PAUL CARBERRY

ENGEN
BOOKS

For my wife, Leah
To fit in with the rest of the books on your shelf

"A reservoir of darkness, black
As witches' cauldrons are, when fill'd
With moon-drugs in th' eclipse distill'd.
Learning to look if foot might pass
Down thro' that chasm, I saw, beneath,
As far as vision could explore,
The jetty sides as smooth as glass,
Looking as if just varnish'd o'er
With that dark pitch in the Sea of Death
Throws out upon its slimy shore."
-HP Lovecraft, The Nameless City

I. Last Day

Percy Benoit leaned against the concrete wall with his arms pressed against the edge hard enough to leave imprints on his forearm. Allen stood at the edge of the stairs next to him, peering down at Percy, unable to watch, as the bat dangled limply from his hands. If Sheldon got on base, Allen would be next, and Percy would be on deck.

On the scoreboard in right field, the dull yellow lights displayed the tied score in the top of the ninth inning: a runner on second base, two outs, and a full count. It all came down to this. If the Crooked Creek Crocodiles batted in one more run, they'd be off to the Atlantic Championships. All they needed to do was beat St. John's, something they hadn't accomplished. Ever.

With his rally cap on, Percy's best friend since first grade, Damien, urged his teammates to join him, cheering from the end of the bench. He shifted his way to Percy, wedging himself between Allen and the stairs. "You gotta win this for us," Damien said, breaking the silence that weighed over the dugout.

Percy shook his head. "James got this."

"That dude always strikes out," Damien answered, drawing an indignant scowl from Allen.

"Didn't you strike out twice this game?" Allen reminded Damien.

"Shut up," the coach snarled from atop the dugout.

The pitcher stepped off the mound, kicking at the dirt, disguising his frayed nerves, buying himself extra time to think. Annoyed, the batter stepped out of the box and hit the bottom of his cleats with the bat; reddish-brown dirt rained down over the grass. James Dempster placed one foot back into the batter's box, holding the bat out in front of him, staring down the barrel, and drew a deep breath. With his composure gathered, he got into his stance, his muscles tense with anticipation.

All around him, the tension built, the crowd buzzing with nervous hope as raucous chatter dissolved into a hushed whisper. With his breath held, Percy's heart raced with anticipation. Unable to handle the pressure, he clenched his eyes shut and waited. The sharp slap of the ball striking leather rang out, followed by the inaudible strikeout call by the umpire. In that instant, a collective gasp deflated the air from the ball field... then the crowd fell silent.

"Take the field," Coach Bergler said, his words jolted by anxiety. "And play aggressive defense. Our season is riding on this."

Percy snatched his glove from the empty bench behind him and trotted up the stairs; the spikes on his cleats clattered off the cement. He made his way to right field, making sure he didn't step on the chalk as he crossed the field. Superstitious nonsense. But he refused to risk it, not in extra innings. He glanced up into the bleachers where his mother was perched in her usual spot. Dead centre behind where Percy played, she waved and blew him a kiss with a warm smile creasing her face.

Embarrassed, Percy's cheeks flushed, but he returned the smile before turning to face home plate. A tense hum reverberated through the crowd as James Holden took the mound. Beads of sweat trickled down his brow. He removed his ball cap and wiped his forehead with it. Nervous, he struggled to locate the strike zone and walked the first batter in four pitches; the crowd fell silent once more.

"You can do this, James," Percy called out, encouraging his pitcher.

James circled the mound, gathering his composure. He drew in a deep breath and stepped back into position. His first pitch thrown was hit sharply into the dirt towards third base. Damien gathered the ball into his glove and threw towards Sheldon on second base. They got the runner out at second, but Damien's wild throw pulled Sheldon out of position and he didn't have time to make an accurate throw; the ball sailed high and wide of the first baseman and the runner advanced to second base on the error.

The crowd didn't know what to do. Some of them clapped, others shouted encouragement, and some of the visiting fans cheered, which forced the home crowd to boo. James gathered the ball, monitoring the runner on second base, trying to hold him there with his glowering gaze. As soon as the first pitch left his hand, he watched it drift towards the battle. It slammed into the opposing player just as he twisted his upper body, trying to protect himself from the impact while still taking the free pass;

the ball smashed into flesh with a dull thud.

James cursed into his glove, trying to conceal his frustration from everyone. The coach waved down the ump. "Time out."

He walked to the mound, joined by the catcher, and they huddled up with James, keeping their voices to a whisper and hiding their mouths as if someone on the St. John's team could read lips. With runners on first and second, the coach gave his best speech to bolster his pitcher's confidence. Before he left, he patted James on the shoulder. "Get him to ground into a double play and the inning is over."

The batter from St. John's stepped into the batter's box and the umpire called for the game to resume. James inhaled, puffing his chest out. Releasing his breath, he wound up and threw the next pitch into the dirt in front of home plate. The ball bounced off the catcher and skittered in the dirt away from him. The base runners advanced to third and second before the catcher could retrieve the ball.

Damien screamed, his words twisted into a jumble of rage and frustration, blending a series of creative curse words into an impressive string of obscenities. Damien's mother urged him to calm down from the crowd, but he ignored her, continuing to insult the mothers from St. John's.

"Watch your tongue, young man," the third base umpire warned Damien. "Or I'll toss you from the game."

Damien drove his cleat into the dirt, kicking a spray of dirt over the chalk line, grumbled to himself but remained calm enough for the umpire to overlook his outburst. The runner on third base laughed at him. "The game isn't over yet," Damien snarled. "I'd wipe that smirk off your face if I were you."

"Play ball," the home plate umpire growled.

James threw the next pitch just outside the strike zone. His third pitch painted the corner. And for an agonizing pause, the umpire built the tension before signaling strike. Whatever he grunted behind the plate didn't sound like a word, instead sounding not much more than a roiling bark.

As James wound up for the next pitch, the batter stepped out of the box before the umpire granted time, and the ball floated over the plate, landing in the catcher's mitt for a no-doubt strike. The batter argued that he called time; but the umpire held up two fingers on each hand, pantomiming the count.

Ready for the next pitch, he swung the bat in an uppercut, driving the ball high and deep to left field. Percy settled a few paces behind the ball, waiting for it to drop from its trajectory, realizing the runner on third would tag up and try to make it home. When the ball began its descent, Percy timed the catch, running into the sinking ball just before it sank below his shoulders. With momentum benefiting him, Percy hurled the ball towards home plate as the runner on third base scampered for home.

The crowd raised to their feet as the ball sailed over the third baseman's head. It landed on the edge of the dirt once, kicking up a splash of reddish soil on its way to the catcher's glove. The base runner slid headfirst towards home plate as Aaron swiped his glove; the umpire crouched low and close to make the call; a cloud of dust rose into the air. From the outfield, Percy watched as the dust settled.

Aaron held his glove up triumphantly, showing the umpire the ball saddled in his catcher's mitt. The runner slapped at home plate, showing where he touched the corner of the plate before Aaron tagged him. Both coaches held their breath, holding the rail running down the stairs to their dugouts. With a flare for the dramatic, the umpire pumped his fist high in the air, calling the base runner out. The crowd exploded as the St. John's coach dashed towards the umpire to argue the call.

Percy glanced over his shoulder, finding his mother's spot empty. He scanned the rambunctious crowd for a sign of her as he trotted back to the dugout. When he reached the stairs, his friends gathered around him, cheering his name and slapping him on the backside.

"You saved my ass," James said, embracing Percy into a bear hug.

"Game's not over yet," the coach interrupted. "We still have work to do."

The players wandered into the dugout, but couldn't settle, the excitement palpable in the air. Percy threw his glove and hat on the bench, grabbed a helmet and bat, and started taking practice swings. Despite the positive vibes in the dug out, Percy's heart raced as Allen made his way to the plate. He studied the pitcher, trying to pick up a sign to help him locate the type of pitch coming next.

Allen flied out to shallow centre field.

Percy stepped into the batter's box, the barrel of the bat resting on his shoulder. The pitcher stared him down, trying to intimidate Percy. As the pitcher began his windup,

Percy kicked his leg, anticipating a fastball; he coiled his muscles and swung. The ball cracked off the bat as a wave of strong vibrations left a euphoric sensation racing up his forearms. Sailing high into the sky, the ball ascended into the sky, soaring for an eternity. Percy admired the trajectory as the ball drifted over the fence.

The ball landed in the vacant spot where his mother should have been. As he trotted around the bases, the home crowd thundered and his teammates gathered at home plate, waiting for him. He ran into the circle, the players all jumping up and down with excitement. Everyone congratulated Percy, hailing him as the town hero for the foreseeable future. Ecstatic, Percy gave up searching the crowd for his mother and joined the celebration. Settled below the pine clad trees, the sun melted from view, with the remnants of daylight fading as the approaching darkness fell from above. A fragment of blue light remained to battle against the invading twilight. A quarter moon suspended in the sky afforded a faint trace of silvery light to the darkening sky. Barely visible, the big dipper constellation emerged, and the North Star twinkled overhead.

Intense flood lights set on an automatic timer powered up, casting a yellow hue over the ball field. Percy heard an orchestra of croaking frogs from the pond behind the home plate bleachers.

Percy remained in the parking lot, watching the cars pull out in a disorganized fashion that could only work in a small town like Crooked Creek. Exhausted from celebrating with his friends, Percy discovered himself alone with his thoughts, which turned back to his mother. His duffel bag stretched out at his feet: bright blue with red trim to match his team's colours. Stuffed into the duffel, the handle of his bat peeked out on one end of the zipper, too long to fit into his bag. Clutched in his hands, he waited for his cell phone to ring. He stared at the screen, hit dial, and let it ring until the voicemail cut in.

"Damn it," Percy mumbled to himself.

"Hey, Percy."

Startled, Percy felt his heart leap into his chest. "You scared me, Coach," Percy said, short of breath.

Coach Bergler stood beside his car with his duffel bag slung over his shoulder. His lip turned up into a snickering smile. "Didn't mean to," he confessed. "Do you have a ride home?" Bergler removed his ball cap. Somehow, his spiked blond hair held in place without the aid of gel.

"Yeah, my mom should be here soon," Percy lied; he did not understand where his mother went.

Bergler opened the door to his truck, the hinges squealing and groaning. He threw his duffel bag into the passenger seat, then turned back towards Percy. "Are you sure, Percy?" His tone was full of concern. "She left before the end of the game. Is everything okay?"

"She got called into work for a moment." It was a convincing lie, considering her profession as a nurse. "But she'll be back any minute now."

Bergler frowned, illustrating his concern for the young man. "Where's your dad?"

"My dad died years ago, Mr. Bergler," Percy responded.

"You know what I meant, Percy," Bergler said, sighing. "Where's Ben?"

"Home would be my guess. Or the bar," Percy added, spitting a wad of phlegm onto the ground.

"You sure you don't need a ride?" Bergler gripped the door, swaying it back and forth. "I'm your last chance."

Percy nodded his head. She could have gotten a call to the hospital and could be stuck there all night; it wouldn't have been the first time that happened, but he found it strange she left saying nothing. He wandered over to the passenger side as the coach slung the bag over the seat and into the back row. "Thanks," Percy said, hauling himself up into the cab of Bergler's truck.

"It's no trouble. I have to drive by your house anyway," Bergler said as he pulled the door closed. The engine sputtered to life, the choking grumble easing into a low rumble. As the truck rolled forward, gravel and rocks popped beneath the tires, and the hinges screeched as they drove over the potholes that littered the dirt parking lot. "In all my years, I've never made it to the Atlantic Championships. Percy, what you accomplished today reaches far beyond the game of baseball. You made Crooked Creek very proud."

Percy felt his cheeks flush with blood, turning his cheeks a rosy red. "I don't know about that, Coach."

"No, I mean it. After those mummer murders last Christmas, this town needed something positive to take the attention away from those horrific tragedies." Bergler flashed his blinker, turning his truck onto the on ramp.

"Hey, Coach," Percy said, surprised. "You're going the wrong way."

"Did you hear any of the details of those crimes?" Bergler continued as if he had never heard Percy speak up. "What we did to that poor girl and her family, you wouldn't believe it. Did you know they held back some of those facts from the press?"

"We?" Percy stared at Bergler.

Bergler accelerated down the highway, leaving his headlights off. The engine roared, and the pedometer swept across the dashboard in. a quick circle. Ignoring Percy's question, Bergler continued, "That girl June and her grandpa put up one hell of a fight, let me tell you."

"Stop the truck, Coach." Percy glanced out the window as the forest flew by in a blur. "I want to get out now, please," he begged.

"Did you know I spread June's guts all over the fireplace mantel?" Bergler laughed. He turned his head towards Percy, taking his eyes off the road. "What's stopping you, kid?"

"You're going too fast," Percy snapped.

Bergler reached over, his sausage-sized fingers outstretched. Percy recoiled, his shoulder bumping against the window; the glass splintered against the impact, and a whistle of wind roared into the cab. "You're free to leave," he cackled, unfastening Percy's seatbelt.

"Are you insane?" Percy spat, forcing his body as tight against the passenger door as possible. "Just let me go, please."

"Nuts?" Bergler slapped his knee and chuckled. "Kid, you do not know. But do you know what's crazy?"

Percy fumbled with the seatbelt, making sure he wouldn't get tangled up in it; he needed to be mobile. Scanning the opposite side of the road, praying for another vehicle he could flag down, he found it barren. All the colour had vanquished from the sky by now, with the moon lurking behind storm clouds giving off only a faint trace of yellow light.

"Your mother is crazy, that's who," Bergler announced.

"Shut your damn mouth," Percy growled. "You don't know my mother."

Bergler's grin widened, pressing his lips against his yellow stained teeth. "Everyone in town knows your mother. Intimately," he added.

"Go to hell." Percy yanked the handle; the door opened before the wind slammed it shut once more. "Fuck!" Percy hollered in frustration and terror. The truck rumbled down the highway at breakneck speed; with no headlights to guide the way, it would only be a matter of moments before the truck careened into a ditch. "You're going to get us both killed," Percy tried to reason with the lunatic.

A set of headlights crested a hill, careening towards them; the shadows along the road narrowing the path of light into a tight cone. Bergler drifted into the oncoming lane, laughing maniacally as Percy reached over, trying to pry his hands from the wheel. Underneath the coach's sweater, Percy felt wiry muscle pull taut and flex. "What the fuck are you doing?" Percy shrieked; tears tracked down his cheek. "You're going to get us killed!"

Without warning, Bergler twisted the wheel hard to the left; the truck rose onto two wheels, drifting across the asphalt before hitting the gravel shoulder. The incoming headlights shined into the cab, casting it in a celestial radiance. Percy shrieked, tucking his head between his legs beneath the dashboard, clenching his eyes shut, but he couldn't shut the light out. Tree branches clattered off the sides of the truck, scratching the panels and battering the windows. The truck heaved up and down, the hinges working overtime as metal bent and groaned against the strain.

"What the hell are you doing?" Percy said, finding his breath.

Silence.

Percy eased his eyes open. Surprised by the brilliant, luminescent light, he rubbed his eyes with the back of his hands. It didn't take long for his eyes to adjust, his pupils constricting to pinpoints. He turned towards the driver's seat, finding it empty; a foul smell wafted in from the open door. His abdomen clenched tight, causing him to dry heave.

Bergler stood in the beam of light, only a silhouette against the sharp halogen lights. His shadowy form motioned for Percy to join him before pointing off into the smothering darkness. He tramped through the shrubs and vanished into the abyss.

Percy pushed his door open, jumped out of the cab onto the soft earth; his shoes sunk into the damp soil. The smell hit him hard. His face twisted into a grimace and he pinched his nostrils shut. He stumbled towards the front of the truck over half-buried roots and tangled branches, using the hood to catch himself. Bergler's footsteps echoed from within the darkness.

"Don't follow," a muffled voice warned.

"Shut your damn mouth," Bergler snarled at the mysterious stranger.

Percy glanced over his shoulder, back towards the highway. Cars whizzed by: the silvery glow from passing vehicles stopped just short of the truck. If he ran, he could make it back to the highway before Bergler could catch him; at least, he thought he could. But something compelled him to follow Bergler into the unknown.

"Please, Percy, you don't need to see this."

Percy cupped his hands over his mouth and yelled out for help. His voice was suffocated by the droning buzz of engines as they raced down the highway. Against his better judgment, Percy wandered towards the edge of the truck's high beams. Above him, tree branches drooped low, forcing him to duck beneath the canopy of fir trees. After stumbling through the thick tapestry, Percy wandered into a clearing. Overhead, the Crooked Feeder Bridge spread across the babbling water: the railing facing Percy bowed outward and split into a mangled gap.

At the centre of the brook, a red Honda Civic, just like his mother's, lay on its hood with the front end collapsed into a tangle of metal and broken glass. Percy stood still, his mouth hanging wide open; the word, 'Mom,' spilled out without a sound. His mind urged him to listen to the strange voice, but his heart refused to listen. His feet trudged forward against his better judgment. Every step brought him closer to the truth. He crouched down low, creeping towards the battered car. Spiderweb cracks made it impossible to see clearly into the interior of the Honda, but it took little convincing to know that anyone in the front seat at the time of the accident wouldn't survive.

"Mom," Percy whispered, desperately trying to convince himself it couldn't be real. Crimson streaks stained the window, running along the web of cracks on the driver's side window.

A scuffling racket caught Percy's attention from behind the car; the sound of heavy breathing and grunting demanded Percy's attention. Slowly, he rose to his feet, peering over the demolished Civic. Bergler cradled his arms beneath a woman's armpits, dragging her into the blackness at the edge of the trees. The woman's face was smashed beyond recognition, a jumble of mangled flesh and gruesome wounds concealing a pair of eyes peeking at Percy behind the mess. Blackened stains ruined the woman's white dress. His mother's dress.

"Mom," a guttural sound escaped Percy's throat as he gave chase into the darkness.

Bergler vanished into the woods with his mother and Percy pursued, fear a transitory memory. Driven into action, Percy raced into the forest without a second thought. Plunged into darkness, his legs kept pumping. Tree branches tore at the flesh on his face, scraping his cheeks and forearms. His foot tangled in a root, and he smashed face first into the hard packed earth and tumbled onto his backside.

He sprang up, panting; and found himself in his bedroom. Percy's eyes wandered around the room, taking it all in as his heart slowed. Another nightmare, he told himself, nothing more. He reached into his nightstand drawer and pulled out the prescription bottle, rattling the remaining pills against the clear orange vial. With a practiced motion, he flipped the lid off with his thumb and dry swallowed the medication. His eyes settled on the red digital display. "Shit," he mumbled as he jumped out of bed and rushed to get his school clothes on.

At least this would be his last day; summer break loomed large at the end of the day. Hopefully the extended break would help him deal with the loss of his mother.

II. School

Half-dressed, Percy sprinted down the road towards the bus stop. With his bookbag slung over his left shoulder, he found himself off balanced for a moment as he tried to slip his right arm into the sleeve of his jacket. A stinging cold persisted from the night before, the June sun too weak in the early morning to dispel the chill. His stomach growled and his head was woozy from the medication: another typical school day since his mother passed. He cursed the doctors who put him on the medication and vowed to stop taking them; they did little to combat the night terrors.

"Hey, Percy," Aaron called out from his front porch as he made his way down the front steps. Out of breath, always a chubby kid even after his growth spurt, Aaron waddled as much as walked towards Percy. "Did you catch the Jay's game last night?"

Percy shook his head, slowing his pace to match Aaron, hearing but not listening as his friend caught him up on last night's game; it was just a jumble of meaningless words to Percy. They reached their bus stop, finding James sitting on the edge of the curb, sifting through his book bag.

"Hey, James," Aaron said, enthusiastic to have a friend to chat about last night's game with.

"Hey guys," James answered, keeping his face buried in his backpack. He rummaged around the bottom, shifting the textbooks back and forth as he searched for some hidden mystery; he cursed under his breath.

"Everything okay, buddy?" Aaron asked James with a heavy look of concern weighing on his face.

"Forgot my math book," James sighed. "I can hear Miss Grace now, 'I sent home a letter, James; there's no reason for you to have forgotten your book.'"

Percy grinned at James' high-pitched impersonation of Miss Grace; but he didn't laugh. Aaron let it all out, chortling and turning red, gasping for breath.

"Why don't you run back and get it?" Percy checked his watch. "You still have five minutes before the bus gets here."

James glanced over his shoulder at his house two lots down and shook his head. "My mom's having a day," he said, leaving it at that.

"You playing baseball this summer, guys?" Aaron asked both boys, but his attention focused on Percy.

James bowed his head. "Better believe it. What else is there to do in this shit hole?"

Everyone laughed, knowing it to be a sad truth.

"What about you, Percy?" James added.

"I don't know," Percy answered. "Maybe."

No one spoke. The gentle melody of the neighborhood waking up disrupted the silence between them, making it bearable. James' dad climbed into his van, driving past the boys with a dismissive wave of the hand. No one waved back. Mr. Thompson started up his lawn mower, the growling roar right on time. You could set your watch on the elderly man's schedule. If the universe had an internal clock, it would defer to the old man's watch.

The bus arrived at the stop sign just around the corner right on time; its diesel engine growled, and the hinges squeaked as the driver made the turn. It rolled past the sign and came to a shuddering stop in front of the boys. They climbed onto the bus. James and Aaron shared an open seat, and Percy wandered down the hall, searching for Damien, knowing he wouldn't be there.

Percy took an empty seat at the back of the bus, and he slung his bookbag onto the seat with a loud thump. Surrounded by a buzz of chatter and excitement, he glared out the window with a vacant expression; an internal struggle occupied his mind as he tried to decide if he would play baseball this summer.

Sweat rolled down Percy's backside. A buzz of excitement electrified the air, making it a chore to remain seated. The babble in the classroom all fused together, synthesizing into a tumultuous melody. Even with the rising racket, every tick of the clock thundered in his ear as the long arm trudged towards twelve. Their teacher, Miss Grace, rustled through her drawer, chewing bubble gum and ignoring the uproarious students. Stacked on the corner of her desk, the last report cards for the school year taunted him. Once he had his in his hand, summer could officially begin; he could smell the pine needles on a warm summers breeze in the outfield.

Since his mother passed away, Percy lost all interest in school; he just wanted to spend the summer playing baseball in the afternoons and camping out at night. Besides, the less time spent with his stepfather, Ben, the better. They never got along, even before his mother died in that car crash.

"Hey, Percy," Damien interrupted Percy's thoughts. "Are you coming with us tonight?" Damien leaned in so close, Percy didn't have to guess what Damien had for lunch. The gang spent last weekend picking out the perfect camping site. Only a twenty-minute ride from Crooked Creek, somehow, they found Deadman's Lake deserted most weekends. With only one abandoned cottage on the far side of the lake, the boys were free to do as they pleased. Nothing was off limits.

"I have to ask my stepfather," Percy answered, struggling not to sound as excited as Damien; a smile slipped across his face. "If he lets me go..."

Damien chuckled, "Man, Ben doesn't care what you do with your time." He rapped his knuckles off his desk. "So, you're in. I'll let the others know you're coming." He hesitated. "They'll come for sure now," he continued.

"Don't get your hopes up," Percy replied, speaking more to himself than Damien.

"Come on, man!" Damien snapped, inviting the wandering eyes of every student in the room. An unnerving silence settled over the classroom. Pressured by the watching eyes, Damien waited for the drone of banter before continuing. "I told Angie you'd be there. If you don't go, she will not bring her friends," he said, rolling his head towards Beth across the classroom. "Please," he begged.

A loud scraping noise cut through the chatter as Miss Grace stood up, the legs of her wooden chair scratching over the worn linoleum. She cleared her throat, allowing the remaining murmurs to silence. "Well, everyone," she began, "I think that it's close enough to dismissal that we can start. Once you have your report card, you're free to leave. I'll see some of you again next year in math class. But for the rest of you, I hope you enjoy your senior year in high school without me." She giggled, smirking.

She swept the report cards into her arms. A collective gasp sucked the air out of the classroom as everyone waited for their name to be called. "Damien," she called out.

Damien bounced up from his seat, clapping Percy on the shoulder. "I'll see you outside, buddy," he said, not waiting any longer. He bolted up front and grabbed his report card. For a moment, he stood still as he examined his marks. A grin creeped across his face as he turned to leave the classroom, pumping his fist into the air before vanishing into the hallway.

Percy sat on the edge of his seat, anxiously awaiting to hear his name announced. Miss Grace called out name after name that wasn't his. Jumbled together, the names became one giant blur until he was the last kid in class. Standing in front of the class with a pleasant smile, Miss Grace called Percy's name in a melodic harmony. He slung his backpack over his right shoulder, bearing the cumulative weight of the entire school year. With a placid smile, he took his report card and headed towards the door.

"Aren't you going to open it?" Miss Grace asked.

Percy stood in the doorway, resting his forearm along the moulding, the corridor eerily quiet for a school day. The raucous clamor of the student body celebrating outside cried out to him.

"We all know you're going through a rough patch, Percy," she stated, her voice soothing. Without looking, Percy knew a pleasant smile remained on her face despite the depressing situation. "I realize you miss your mom, and your grades will come back up next year." She spoke with a motherly tenderness that made him miss his mom. A tear welled up in the corner of his eye that Percy refused to let her see. "I believe in you," she added.

Discreetly, he wiped the tear away, "Thank you."

"Enjoy your summer," she said, her tone full of optimism and joy.

"You too," Percy said. Now, in the vast emptiness of the corridor, Percy opened his report card. "Damn it," he muttered out loud, stuffing the card into his book bag. A sense of dread fell over him. He felt his summer slipping away. Hopefully, Ben would be in one of his better moods when he got home.

Alone, Percy trudged down the sidewalk; his mind was distant. Cars cruised past, houses came and went, birds chirped and fluttered between the trees, but Percy kept his head down. He should have been excited. Summer break sprawled before him; limitless possibilities awaited him; he should have raced home without a care in the world. Instead, he wandered aimlessly through town, no longer heading home and not knowing why.

A thunderous crack rang out, the familiar sounds of the bat drawing Percy's attention. He glanced up, surprised by the sight of the freshly cut grass and chalked foul lines alongside the ballfield. The ball landed with a dull thump in the left field, sinking into the still damp field. From the pitcher's mound, James waved at him with a beaming smile plastered on his face.

"Hey Percy," James called out, running to the fence. "Do you want to play? We could use another body."

Reluctantly, Percy made his way over to the fence. "Not today, maybe tomorrow if you guys are playing," he mumbled.

"Are you sure?" James asked, the bat dangling from his hand, clanking off the fence as the other boys gathered.

"I didn't even bring my glove," Percy lied; he always packed his glove in his bookbag.

"Actually," Allen piped up from the back, "team tryouts are tomorrow. You're coming, right, Percy?"

"If we want to make it back to the championships again, we're going to need you," Sheldon added.

"I don't know," Percy grumbled, wanting to leave.

"He won't show up," James said, clunking the top of the bat off the ground, punctuating his disappointment.

Everyone except James left the fence and returned to the field.

"I'm just not ready. Our last game was the last time I ever remember seeing my mother," Percy explained. It felt good to say it out loud, like a burden was lifted from his shoulders.

"I'm sorry," James sympathized. After an awkward silence between them, James spoke up. "I should get back to the game." He held up the bat. "They're waiting for me."

"Have fun," Percy said, feeling at a loss for words.

"You should come out tomorrow. Even if you don't play, everyone would love to see you," James said. He didn't give Percy a chance to respond before ambling away.

Percy reached out, his fingers gripping the top bar of the fence. His vision strolled across the field, taking it all in. When his eyes fell on the left field bleachers, they fixated on his mother's spot. He could see her plain as day, waving back at him. Her white dress billowed in the wind, her greying hair dancing with the breeze. For the first time in a long time, Percy's imagination didn't conjure up a gruesome depiction of his mother.

Percy stayed for a few pitches before heading home.

The door banged shut downstairs, jarring Percy's concentration away from his respite in the Marvel Universe. He drifted across his bed and peeked out his bedroom window. His stepfather's archaic Ford pickup was parked in the driveway on a slant. Bags filled with cans thumped off the counter.

"Hey, Percy!" Ben hollered. "If you're home, come help me put away these damn groceries."

Percy dropped the Spider-Man comic back into the box and slid it underneath his bed. With his stomach in knots, he trudged down the stairs; they creaked and groaned. Standing at the kitchen sink, Ben drained a can of beer and rinsed it out, keeping the faucet running as he grabbed another beer from the fridge. His white tank top was stained with black grease and sweat, and more of the black gunk smudged his khaki shorts. He had a leather tool belt dangling from his hip, the intense yellow shaft of his hammer hung low like a cowboy's revolver. It made him look ridiculous. Despite what Ben thought about himself, he would never be that cool. After three deep gulps, Ben belched, used the stainless steel of the sink to crumple the can before he rinsed it out, shutting off the faucet.

With nothing to say, Percy got to work putting away the cans in the lower cupboards. If he didn't, he knew Ben would explain to him how bad his lower back was; Percy had grown sick of that narrative and wasn't in the frame of mind to listen to the same old song and dance.

"What are you doing home so early on a school day?" Ben asked, incredulous. He opened the fridge, bent at the hip to search the second shelf. After moving around some Tupperware containers, he found another cold one.

"They let us go early because it's the last day of school," Percy sighed. He sensed Ben's wicked hazel eyes staring a hole into the back of his head.

"No need for your damn sauce today boy." Ben slammed the aluminum can down onto the counter, punctuating his point.

"Well, don't you want to read my report card?" Percy suggested, his voice timid.

"Is this what you're trying to show me?" Ben yanked it out of his front pocket. "I picked it up when I came in the house," he announced, tossing it in the garbage can. "That pathetic excuse for a report card." He brandished an accusing finger at Percy. "You better get your marks up, boy," he snapped. "Your mother would have cried her eyes out if she were alive for this."

"What are you so furious about? If I remember correctly, you're a high school dropout," Percy snapped, the pent-up frustrations rising to the surface.

Flushed red with rage, Ben's features twisted into a sinister aberration. The veins on his forehead and neck bulged. "Watch your damn mouth," he growled.

Percy held back a fit of hitching sobs, tears streaked down his cheek. Anger filled his body, making him shudder. "I passed," he grumbled.

"You won't get any scholarships with these grades." He thudded his fist against the kitchen counter. "And if you think I'm paying for you to run off to university," he chortled, "you're sadly mistaken."

"Whatever," Percy muttered, shaking his head.

"This is your last warning; do you understand me, you little punk?" Ben thrust his finger at Percy, driving it into his chest.

Percy's body unleashed a wave of emotions in a tidal flood, washing over him; he felt like he was fighting against raw hatred, his head far beneath the surface, struggling to catch his breath. "I'm heading to the library," he lied, shoving his feet into his sneakers.

"You don't actually expect me to believe that," Ben laughed. "I might not have finished school, but I'm not stupid."

Percy lost his temper and threw the door open; the hinges squealed, and the frame rattled. "I don't care!" Percy screamed, slamming the door behind him. Ben's harsh howl chased after him. He raced into the backyard, dashing behind the corner just as Ben stormed out of the house.

"You get back here!" Ben shouted, running to the end of the driveway, his bare feet slapping off the pavement.

Percy watched Ben turn left and stormed down the road in the opposite direction of the library. He sprinted across the yard and jumped the fence into the neighbouring property with practiced ease. His legs pumped, carrying him in the library's direction. The landscape all around him blurred into a haze. Before he realized it, he was standing on Damien's front porch. He rang the doorbell, peering over his shoulder. Fear gripped his heart, expecting to discover Ben lumbering towards him at any moment.

"Hey, Percy," Damien greeted him, stepping outside and embracing Percy in a bear hug. "You're here early. Could it be that you 're eager to go camping? Or do you just want to see Angie that bad?"

"Can I just come inside, please?" Percy asked politely, even as he elbowed his way past his friend.

"Are you doing okay?"

"Close the door," Percy ordered, standing in the porch's corner, half concealed within the closet.

"Did Ben lose his temper at you?" he asked, but didn't have the compassion to wait for an answer. "Are you going with us tonight?" Damien closed the door and turned the lock.

As it thumped into place, a flood of relief washed over him. "Furious," he responded. "And hell yeah."

III. Beer Run

Captured in the clouds, the dying sunlight turned the sky a salmon pink. Percy leaned against the cinderblock wall, his eyes dashing back and forth across the street. Damien perched on the curb, his knapsack tucked between his legs. Pale yellow light washed across the parking lot as a car pulled in, casting their elongated shadows across the liquor store facade.

"That's our guy," Damien said, enthusiasm driving him to his feet. "So please go ask him before he runs inside."

"I don't know," Percy hesitated.

"You claimed you wanted to fit in with us," Damien replied, accusing him. "When are you going to do that?" he added.

The red Civic pulled into a parking spot along the front of the store; the engine knocked and sputtered in idle. When the driver eventually killed the ignition, the motor continued to knock and rattle. The rusted hinges of the door groaned loudly as the driver shoved it open.

"When are you going to grow a set, man?" Damien pleaded, his hands tented below his chin. "I promised the girls we'd get them their coolers."

"Fine," Percy grumbled under his breath. He shuffled around the corner, his sneakers grinding over the dusty pavement. Inside he was a bundle of nerves. Sweat formed on his brow in beads, his cheeks flushed red with embarrassment. Determined to fit in and impress his friends, he gathered his courage, puffed out his chest, and ordered his legs to move. Without thinking, he wandered in front of the building and stood at the entrance; the automatic door slid open with a pneumonic swishing noise.

"Hey, kid," the stranger said, laughing. "You mind stepping aside if you're not going in. Some of us have places to go tonight?" The man swept his hand through his long, chestnut brown hair. Unkempt and straggly looking, he gave off a college student vibe. He wore a Pink Floyd t-shirt tucked into a worn pair of denim jeans.

Percy's mouth opened, but the words caught in his throat. A strange stuttering groan escaped. Not knowing what to do, he stood there like a deer in the headlights. He crammed his hands into his pockets, hauling out a wad of crumpled cash, holding it there.

A smirk spread across the man's face, exposing a thin line of white between his lips. "You want me to buy you liquor?" the guy suggested.

Percy nodded his head. A lump formed in his throat, and he swallowed it down; his Adam's apple bobbed up and down. "It's only because I forgot my ID at home, you know," he whispered.

"Christ, kid," the man grumbled. He reached out, grabbing Percy by the elbow, and dragged him around the corner of the building. "If you want to get yourself caught, standing in the entrance trying to hand over cash to strangers has got to be the quickest way."

Damien sighed, rubbing the bridge of his nose. "Can you help us, mister? Please," he added.

The man tapped his foot off the pavement, his worn shoe thumping on the ground. "What's in it for me, kid?" the stranger inquired.

"What do you want from us?" Damien replied, irritated. "Don't stand there and pretend you never asked someone to help buy you booze when you were a kid."

The man raised his hands in the air and waved them down and away. "I don't need this," he spat, turning to walk away.

Percy reacted without reasoning. His hand reached out and grasped the man's wrist, twisting him around. "I can pa... pay... pay you," he sputtered.

"Re... real... really?" the man mocked Percy, glaring down at him; his eyes ignited with impatience. With a violent tug, the man freed his arm from Percy's clutch.

Ignoring the insult, Percy continued. "I'll pay you twenty bucks." He reached into his back pocket and hauled out another crumpled bill.

The man's glare dissolved, and he smirked. "How old are you?"

"Eighteen," Percy lied.

"Bullshit," the stranger laughed. "But I guess it doesn't matter. You're definitely not nineteen." He reached out and snatched all the money. "Just tell me what you want, and I'll grab it for you as long as it isn't a hassle."

"A six pack of coolers and a dozen bud light," Percy answered, rhyming off his list from the top of his head.

"And a flask of rum," Damien added, grinning from

ear to ear.

The man nodded his head, tucked the wad of bills into his front pocket, and headed towards the front door without speaking another word. For a moment, Percy expected the stranger to jump into his car and take off with all the money. Then the automatic door glided open, and Percy realized he'd been holding his breath.

Percy's forearms ached from carrying the case of beer; the veins ran over his wrists in deep rivulets. With every step, the bottles rattled and clanked together. A breeze whistled through the summer leaves, carrying the fragrant aroma of the deep forest. "Why did I have to carry this the long way around?"

"Well, dummy," Damien began, his tone sarcastic. "We couldn't walk up main street carrying a case of beer."

"What I meant was, why did *I* have to carry it?" Percy asked, placing a great deal of emphasis on the subject.

Damien chuckled before answering, "I thought you could use a little work on those scrawny arms. After all, you're trying to impress Angie, aren't you?"

"Fuck off," Percy grunted. "Please, I need a break before I drop this case and break everything inside."

"Fine," Damien spat.

"Hey losers," an authoritative, booming voice called out from the trail behind them. "What's that you got there?"

Startled, Percy gasped, sucking in a deep breath, and twisted around before Damien had control over the box of beer, and the cardboard separated at the corner. A tearing sound ripped through the silent forest before being drowned out by the clatter of glass bottles.

"Percy!" Damien shouted, demanding his friend's attention.

But Percy felt compelled to run. Without turning to face Damien, his legs tensed, ready to carry him into the woods before the stranger could get a better look at him. Just as he turned to run, he heard familiar laughter.

"Calm down, chicken shit," Adam said, laughing. "I don't want you breaking any beer."

When Percy looked over, Adam and Edward stood dead centre on the trail. A red cooler hung in the air between them with each boy holding onto the handle on either side. "Good thing we're not the cops. We could hear you coming from a mile away."

"Aren't you following us?" Damien asked them, a flare of anger in his voice.

"Get over it," Edward said as he walked in tandem with Adam.

"Stick the beer in here," Adam offered as they placed the cooler on the trail. "That box won't last ten more feet." Adam flipped the lid open, revealing two bags of ice. He took them out, laying them on the ground beside the cooler. "Let's go before the girls get bored and leave."

"Is Angie going to be there?" Percy asked, trying to hide the nervousness beneath a tone of indifference. Glass clanked together as they placed the beer into the coolers.

"Yeah, dude, she is," Edward answered as he broke open a bag of ice with a loud pop and dumped it into the cooler.

Adam shoved the second bag on top and slammed the lid shut before an adult strolled past and take a sneak peek inside. Both boys groaned as they hoisted the cooler

off the ground, and the gravel crunched and skittered beneath their feet as they started back down the trail.

"Don't worry, boys, we're almost there," Damien
said.

"Easy for you to say," Edward complained through
clenched teeth.

"You're not the one carrying this damn thing," Adam
added.

Fluttering with butterflies, Percy's stomach spasmed
at the thought of running into Angie outside of school.
He didn't know what to say; and he didn't know how to
act. "So… what's the plan?" Percy asked, a clear sense of
dread rattled his words.

"Get drunk?" Damien laughed. "What do you
mean?"

"Don't worry about it," Percy exhaled.

"Is this your first time drinking?" Astounded, Damien
stopped dead in his tracks.

"No," Percy said bluntly, not bothering to mention
that he'd only drank Ben's beer alone in his own room
after his step-father passed out. Not waiting for Damien
to pry any further, Percy trudged down the trail towards
the beach.

"I just assumed—" Damien began, then halted.

"Assumed what?" Percy snapped.

"You know," Damien said, his arms framing his face
with his palms facing up.

"Don't go there, dude," Edward groaned.

"Because your father's a drunk," Damien said, oblivious to the mean nature of his own comment.

"Oh, come on, Damien," Adam added his two cents.

"What? If my mother just went missing and my father drank his life away, I'd sneak a beer or two."

"You're an asshole sometimes," Adam said, shaking his head in disgust.

Stunned, Percy stared down at his feet and balled his hands into fists before stuffing them into his pockets. Saying nothing, Percy pushed the branches aside and stepped out onto the craggy shore of Deadman's Creek. Knots twisting in his stomach as he noticed Angie's smile greeting him.

"Hey!" Angie called out, waving her hand for him to come over. "You actually showed up. I didn't believe Damien when he said you were coming."

"That's what she said," Damien whispered loud enough for the boys to hear as he passed Percy and patted him on the backside, his hand guiding Percy towards the beach... and towards Angie. All the resentment towards Damien flooded out of Percy in a burst of giggling laughter; Adam and Edward joined him.

A curious smile crossed Angie's face, distracted by the laughter. "What's so funny?"

"Just stupid guy stuff," Damien answered.

"Nothing to give a second thought," Percy said, nodding his head and accepting his friend's apology.

Angie gave a thumbs up, her smile fading with the sun. Silhouetted by the glossy dark surface of Deadman's Lake, Angie's jet-black hair integrated into the water; her rosy complexion stood out against the mysterious chasm of the black water. Her smile exposed dimples in her cheek, her eyes inviting, while cardinal lipstick added a touch of elegance far beyond her years.

Adam and Edward explored for a spot to place the cooler, trampling around the beach until they found a flat enough area. Once they found a suitable spot, they eased the cooler down and both breathed a sigh of relief. Adam took a seat on the cooler, resting his elbows on the inside of his knees, and placed his head between his lanky fingers.

"Beth should be here soon," Angie said, checking her cell phone. The soft glow illuminated her delicate features. "We should build a fire before it gets too dark."

"You two go gather the wood," Adam said, his words muffled by his hands as he spoke through them.

"Yeah," Edward said, breathing heavy. "We just lugged the cooler all the way here. It's only fair."

"Come on, Percy," Damien said, catching Percy off guard. He expected Damien to complain and put up a fight before conceding. "Let's go."

IV. Stories Around the Fire

The fire cast a hazy radiance over the beach, reflecting off the black surface of the water. The flames devoured the dry wood in the crisp night air. Percy and his friends gathered around the blaze in a relaxed circle. A few brave flies buzzed around his head, determined to get one last ounce of blood before the smoke forced them to stay away.

Angie stood beside her friend across the fire from Percy, giggling as they exchanged words he couldn't quite pick out. But he realized they were speaking about him when both girls' eyes fixed on Percy, judging him.

Damien strolled over to Percy with a mischievous grin plastered on his face and an amber bottle grasped by the neck in each hand. "Beer?"

A hesitant smile creased Percy's face. "I'm not thirsty," Percy chuckled, trying to cloak the high-pitched note of his voice. Mixing beer with his pills ended badly every time; he didn't want to make a fool of himself in front of Angie.

"You don't drink beer to quench your thirst," Damien replied. He held out the bottle for Percy to take and leaned in close. "Everyone else is drinking. Don't be a pussy."

With a profound sigh, Percy snatched the bottle

from Damien and took a swig. Surprised by the taste, he coughed, making a spray of foamy beer squirt between his pressed lips. "It's warm," Percy snorted. If Ben could be famous, it would be his uncanny ability to keep his beer ice cold.

Everyone laughed. Percy felt Angie's eyes on him; he took another gulp, forcing the warm bubbles down his throat to impress the group. Damien patted him on the backside as the beer sloshed around in his empty stomach.

"That's what happens when you have to rely on the kindness of strangers," Damien said with a smile. "Dude grabbed a case from the floor instead of picking up one from the cooler."

"They'll be cold soon enough," Edward spoke up from the other side of the fire. "I took them out of that cooler Adam brought and stuck them into the Lake. They'll be ready to drink in no time."

"My cooler's not good enough?" Adam protested, offended.

"How did you know to do that?" Damien asked for the group.

"My father does it all the time," Edward replied matter-of-factually.

"Hey, who knows any spooky ghost stories?" Beth spoke up, her tone exasperated and bored. She sipped her vodka cooler from a straw, her candy red lipstick leaving stains on the yellow plastic.

"Gather around, children," Adam laughed. "I've got one that will leave you breathless."

"This better not be about the time your mom came to

school without makeup on." Everyone burst out laughing at Edward's ingenious remark. "I don't want to have those nightmares again," Edward continued before the laughter died.

"Shut up, Eddy!" Adam snapped. "Do you want to hear the story of the cottage across the lake?"

"This one always gives me the creeps," Damien said, nudging Percy with his elbow.

"Give it a whirl, Adam, though it's probably not that scary." A smirk crept across Beth's face. "But it's not like you losers are saying anything else interesting."

For a moment, Percy felt a wave of nausea wash over him; he wasn't sure if it was the beer or the thought of Angie leaving with her friend. Edward threw an armful of fallen branches on the fire. The flames engulfed the twigs with a *whumpf* and sent a hypnotizing display of red-hot flankers dancing in the air.

"Everyone who lives in Crooked Creek has heard the stories floating around about what happened to the previous owners," Adam started.

"The wife hung herself after drowning her husband in Deadman's Lake. So cliche," Beth sighed.

"You're talking about the legend of Deadman's Lake," Adam said. The flames cast flickering shadows across his face as he leaned towards the centre of the blazing fire. "Everyone knows that story. I'm talking about the original occupants. Before the woman who hung herself ever moved to Crooked Creek."

"Oooh," Angie cooed. "I don't think I've ever heard that story before." Angie tilted her bottle of Smirnoff Ice back; the liquid sloshed around inside, showing that she had finished her drink. "Does anyone want the bottom?"

"Percy will try it," Damien answered, not giving anyone else a chance.

"Here you go," Angie said, thrusting the bottle into Percy's chest.

The glass bottle thumped against Percy's chest, and a sickly sweet aroma rose from the slender opening. Percy stared down at the bright white liquid inside, his taste buds already sensing the sweetness before hitting his tongue. Against his better judgment, he tilted his head back and drowned the rest in two giant gulps. This accelerated the growing sense of light-headedness that clouded his judgement.

"Before my grandfather passed away years ago, he used to tell me this story about the Indians that lived over there," Adam said, his right index finger thrust towards the cottage as if accusing it of something.

"I think you mean Indigenous Canadians," Beth cut Adam off, her tone biting. "You don't have to be so ignorant."

Curious, Percy stepped closer into the circle so he could see Adam better through the flames. The fire crackled; a knot of wood sizzled and shot out of the fire in a blistering whir of red flankers. Landing in the water, the knot fizzled out in the ice cold drink. Percy turned towards the darkness, using the shadows to conceal the grimace on his face as he took another swig of the warm Bud Light. The heat from the fire singed the hairs on his legs. But the alcohol numbed his sense of pain.

"Yeah," Adam said, his voice weak with embarrassment. "I meant nothing by it."

"Go on with your story," Percy interjected. "I'd like to hear this."

"Umm, so where was I?"

"You were about to tell us your grandfather's story," Angie answered. Somehow, she had gotten herself another cooler from the shadows.

It made Percy wonder where the girls were keeping their drinks and just how many they had; it seemed like they had an unending supply tucked away.

"Right. So, my grandfather said that the man who lived in the cottage was a shaman. Very spiritual, you know, a healer. And nature lover." Adam leaned in closer to the fire, the quivering flames lashing out for a taste of his flesh as he dropped a log into the centre. Veiled in the darkness, an owl hooted over the sound of the crackling fire as it engulfed the fresh fuel.

"You're going to say the Shaman put a curse on that place. Is that it?" Each word was interwoven with sarcasm from Beth's lips.

"Do you have to ruin the story?" Edward snapped. "Can't you just let him tell it without interrupting him?"

"Whatever," Beth replied in an uninterested drawl.

Percy took another long drink of beer, draining it before Adam could continue. "Anyone else want another one?"

"That's my boy," Damien smiled, slapping Percy on the back with a firm strike. Percy stumbled forward and tumbled towards the fire, tripping in his own feet; the heat of the fire rushed towards him. But before he fell in, Edward grasped Percy around the waist and hauled him backwards.

"Maybe you let me get this round," Edward said, holding back both Percy and a fit of laughter.

"Let me get it," Damien offered. "I could use a break from the heat." Damien stumbled into the shallow water, his feet scuffing through the rocks beneath the surface. "Does anyone else want one?"

"I do," Adam responded. "All this story telling is making my throat dry."

A moment later, Damien appeared with four bottles of beer for all the boys and distributed them. Adam held his bottle out, tilting the bottom outwards. Percy noticed that the other boys clanged the bottom of their bottles together, so he joined in. A flood of euphoria, mixed with the alcohol, gave him a light head; he wobbled in place, his knees loose and unsteady.

Once everyone had clicked their bottles together, Adam held his beer up over his head. "To summer," he toasted.

Edward added, "Despite Mother Nature's unwillingness to cooperate."

Everyone shared a laugh, and Percy tilted his head back, taking a deep swig of the beer. He found it went down much smoother cold; it went down smoother and didn't upset his stomach. For a moment, he could understand why Ben kept so many silver cans in the refrigerator. After taking another gulp, Percy responded, "To summer."

"You boys," Beth groaned and rolled her eyes. "You should toast poor decisions and regret."

"Oh, stop it," Angie giggled. "You're terrible, Beth."

With a mischievous smile, she stole Percy's breath. He

stared at her, their eyes meeting over the fire as the flames kissed her face. She brought the glass bottle up to her lips, tilting the bottle back while matching Percy's gaze. Percy blushed, lost his courage, and shifted his gaze down at his feet. Nervous, he kicked at the rocks underneath his feet and cursed at himself under his breath.

"Enough of this, lets get back to my story," Adam declared in a booming, theatrical voice. It took a moment for the girls to stop guffawing amongst themselves. When they did, Adam continued his story.

"Before the railroad passed through this area, before Crooked Creek built up around it, the only people to live in this area built their homes around the lake. There were four families that lived here in peace for years. First, the government used the giant trees in this area to build ties for the railroad."

"And this upset the Shaman?" Angie interrupted.

"It did," Adam answered without breaking stride. "He made a formal protest that a judge squashed in the St. John's courthouse after a two-day hearing. Defeated, the Shaman came back to his home, and the loggers moved their equipment into the area."

"We all know this part," Beth said. "Everyone knows Crooked Creek's origin. We're told it every year on family day. 'The little town that could'."

Everyone laughed, even Adam. "You know the story they tell. What you don't know," Adam paused. "Is the actual truth behind how the town became so crooked."

"You know," Edward spoke up, "those murders last Christmas by the mummers... My mom said the investigators had a theory that the people who orchestrated the

murders are from away. No natural born Newfoundland-
er would ever dream of doing something so vicious."

"I believe that it's a cult," Angie added.

"Can we get back to my story? We can tell the mummer story after."

"Let him finish. And the sooner the better," Beth spoke
with disinterest.

"Right," Adam sighed. "So anyway, left with no other
choice, the Shaman sabotaged the logging equipment. At
first, no one knew it was him. But when it kept happening,
the men working in the forest realized that it had to be a
person messing with their tools and machines."

"What did they do?" Percy asked. The words felt
strange on his tongue, rolling together and slurred. Suddenly, his knees unhinged, and he lost his balance. The
beer inside the bottle sloshed around, a frothy foam
spewed from the neck.

Damien leaned in close to Percy and whispered into
his ear, "Ease up a little."

Percy shoved Damien back with a grunt. "I want to
know what happened," he said, turning to Adam. "Finish
your story."

Adam laughed and shot Edward a sideways glance.
"Well, as we all know, the law in these parts is pretty thin
— especially back then. So the loggers took matters into
their own hands."

"So he cursed them," Beth drawled. "Typical."

"Let Adam finish," Percy snapped.

Beth withdrew from Percy, staring at him with her
nose scrunched up and her eyes wide with surprise. Not
understanding where the outburst came from, regret

flushed through his system; he stared into his bottle, not knowing why. Searching for answers, he felt compelled to apologize. But he couldn't think of anything to say; instead, he swayed in place.

After a moment of silence, Adam continued. "No, he didn't. Never got the chance, even if he wanted to. They tore out some beams from the cabin in his basement, tied him to them, and threw him in the lake."

"Why would they do that?" Angie asked.

"Because he loved nature so much, I guess. Maybe they were trying to be ironic or some shit." Adam paused, taking a drink in the dead silence. When he tilted his bottle down, the beer swirled against the bottom, foaming up. "And here's where things get weird."

"They're kinda strange already," Damien joined in the conversation for the first time.

"So far, they've just been cruel," Beth spoke up.

Adam nodded his head and said, "For once tonight, Beth, I agree with you." They exchanged warm smiles: a release of tension between them.

"There has to be something more to this story?" Beth asked, taking a sip of her cooler waiting for Adam to continue.

"Of course," Adam laughed. "This is where shit goes sideways. They say that the Shaman's wife, stricken with grief, retrieved her husband's corpse from the bottom of the lake and buried him beneath the cottage. Apparently, she laid his body to rest beneath the missing beams."

"So he haunts the place?" Percy asked, confused.

"Not exactly," Adam said, drawing out his words.

"Then what is it?" Percy asked impatiently; he needed

another beer.

"They say that the Shaman's spirit infects anyone it comes in contact with."

"Just don't go into the cottage and you'll be fine?" Damien said, his gaze shifting towards the cottage across the lake.

Adam shook his head. "It's not that simple. They say that his spirit lives on amongst the trees that grew from the soil that his rotting corpse fertilized."

"So don't play in the bushes?" Damien jested. Everyone laughed.

"I wish it were that simple," Adam said as he knelt down by the fire, his face cast in an orange glare. "My grandfather told me the wife would uproot the trees and plant them all around Crooked Creek. That's the reason so many terrible things happen here. Evil roots grow deep." He poked at the fire with a stick, and a cluster of flankers danced into the night sky, swirling out over the lake. The embers hissed and sizzled out as they landed on the surface of the lake.

"Jesus," Beth said as she held her hand over mouth. "You're telling me his wife spread the curse?"

"Not exactly," Adam answered with a flare in his voice.

"What do you mean?" Percy asked, needing to understand the answer.

"She thought that's what he would have wanted, to be one with nature. But she didn't realize that his soul had soured and festered into a wicked spirit."

"And the worst part is," Edward said with a sly grin, "we may have just burned some of his essence and released it into the air."

"Stop," Beth blurted. "You're freaking me out."

"Don't worry, Beth," Adam said in a gentle tone. "Fire is the only thing that keeps his spirit away."

"Hey," Damien interrupted, "I got a tale I that I think you'll all like."

The crackling fire burned on the beach as the flames mirrored back off the lake's placid surface. Percy stumbled towards the water and waded out towards the bottles immersed in the chilly waters of Deadman's Lake with his bottle of pills clutched in his fist. With practiced ease, he flicked the cap off and dumped the pills into the black waters. "Good riddance," he muttered to himself. Under the influence of alcohol, he couldn't think of a good enough reason to keep taking them; they had only been holding him back, keeping him down. He held up a can of beer, admiring it with a thin smile.

"Does anyone else want one?" he called out. The only response given was a chorus of raucous, drunken laughter. When he bent over, a glimmer of light caught his attention, and he toppled face first into the lake. Somehow, his hands broke his fall, and he didn't break any of the glass bottles.

On his hands and knees, he strained his neck to peer across Deadman's Lake. A beam of yellow light cut through the upstairs window of the abandoned cottage. The peculiar sight drew his attention. It had been years since anyone stepped foot inside that cottage. No one from Crooked Creek would be foolish or brave enough to venture into that cursed cottage; not after years of the local rumor mill spiraled out of control. The mythology of

Deadman's Lake stretched long and expanded across the paranormal spectrum, ranging from ghosts to demonic possession; not a single resident of Crooked Creek knew the truth. Damien's story won the award for the funniest story of the night. Edward brought home the trophy for the grossest. But Adam's tale chilled him to the bone. He couldn't push it out of his mind. Every time he tried to think about something else, his mind would wander back to the phrase *"roots of evil."*

They had all taken turns weaving spooky stories about the lake or the town. But none of them gave him the shivers like Adam's had. Percy couldn't help but wonder if his mother had gotten tangled in the roots of evil. Or if her rotting corpse fed them. He remembered his mother telling him about the time her friends dared her to spend a night in the cottage. She bragged about surviving the night and hearing voices emanating from within the walls. Now he believed spending the night within those walls had infected her with the Shaman's curse.

Maybe she had passed the curse to him.

The derelict cottage on the far shore seemed to grow large and loom in front of Percy now. A flash of fiery red hair dashed across the front patio. The flashlight burned, the beam bounced up and down, then shot straight down. A woman raised her arm to shield her face from the light, and she turned her head towards Percy. In that moment, Percy froze, wondering if the girl caught him staring at her. She brandished an affectionate smile towards him, her emerald eyes examining him.

"Percy," Angie called out, her voice a soft, angelic coo. "Did you fall into the lake?"

Everyone guffawed. Percy's attention snapped back to the fire. When he glimpsed over his shoulder at the cottage, he discovered it lurking in the twilight far away, silhouetted against the forest. It must have been his mind playing tricks on him. "No," he called back, staring out across the lake. The black reflective surface was darker than the night sky, threatening to devour him whole.

Someone trudged through the shallow waters towards him, their feet slapping towards him. "You okay?" Damien said, snickering. He held out his hand, helping Percy to his feet. "Come join us, you fool." He slurred his words together: *"Commons, ya fool."*

Percy twisted the cap off the beer, tossing it into the darkness. Whatever he experienced earlier had vanished. A silvery moonlight highlighted the decrepit frame of the cottage across the lake. His mind, corrupted for the first time by alcohol, must have been playing a malicious trick on him. At least, that's what he told himself as he shuffled back to the fire.

"You're soaking wet." Beth smiled. "Either you pissed yourself, or you fell in."

"Beth," Angie said, embarrassment raised the pitch of her voice. "Stop it. Percy's going to leave if you keep picking on him."

"I tripped," Percy defended himself.

"Well," she started, taking a tentative step towards him. "I'm just glad you're okay."

Percy's face flushed red with embarrassment. He took a deep swig from the amber bottle, trying to buy himself enough time to think of something to say. A wave of nausea sloshed around inside his belly, and he felt like he was going to throw up. The effects of alcohol hit him like a truck: unexpected and defenseless against its will.

"Are you okay?" Angie asked, rubbing her hand over his shoulder.

Everything in his vision spun; he became woozy. The fire blurred into the darkness until the night sky appeared to be on fire. All the stars tinted red by the flames, thousands of smouldering embers appeared, raining down on them. Bile rose into the back of his throat, and he covered his mouth with the palm of his hand.

"Why don't you sit down," Angie suggested.

"Hey buddy," Damien's voice emerged out of thin air. "Easy does it."

Before Percy could protest, Damien and Angie guided him towards a lawn chair. He observed their lips moving in silent speech; they were talking back and forth. Their faces loomed over him, hovering over him. Slouched in the chair, the background continued to spin around his friends, making him dizzy. A stinging wind cut across the lake, driving their voices away. Hopeless to fight against it, he closed his eyes, trying to force the world to settle. The fire roared in his ear, drowning out the sound of his friends. He watched the stars spiraling in his vision as he drifted helplessly towards a restless state of semi-consciousness.

Before he plunged into oblivion, he could hear a familiar voice singing to him. Beautiful, the song was reminiscent of a lullaby his mother used to sing to him whenever he fell ill. With a recognizable voice serenading him, he embraced the darkness awaiting him. Desperate for her love, he dreamed of his mother singing to him as the wind from the cottage across the lake whispered into Percy's ear.

The woman in white fled across the beach, and Percy followed. Locks of fiery red bounced off her shoulder as she sprinted towards Deadman's Lake. Rocks skittered across the shore, her bare feet kicking them behind her. Dipping low in the sky, the setting sun settled behind the mountains. Darkness crept into the horizon, devouring the sunlight, and casting the lake in deep shadows and brilliant highlights. Without faltering, the woman ran over the lake, her footsteps never once causing more than a ripple on the glassy surface.

With no time to question what had just happened, Percy followed her path. Arcs of water splashed up all around him, soaking through his jeans and swallowing his legs as the water deepened. But he kept trudging through the water until it reached his waist. Not able to keep pace, Percy watched helplessly as the woman glided across the mirrored surface, making her way across without a single drop of water finding its way onto her dress.

"Mom!" Percy called out, desperate and out of breath. "Wait for me."

He waded out into the black water up to his chest; the icy cold water turning his blood to sludge in his veins and filling his muscles. From the depths of the lake, a series of roiling bubbles burst through the tranquil surface. Each air pocket burst with a gurgled, choking scream that froze Percy in his tracks. Thick globs of crimson floated on the surface, and white worms slithering through the viscous fluids squirmed towards Percy. Frightened, Percy back peddled towards the shore. A fetid, coppery stench filled

Percy's nostrils, reminding him of decaying flesh: maggots.

"I need you to come home!" Percy cried. He stood upon the shore, petrified and confused; tears of frustration and anger tracked down his cheeks. "Why won't you come back?"

An ethereal glow engulfed his mother as she strode along the shore. Her pale skin shone as radiant as the stars overhead. From deep within the woodland, a guttural growl roared at the rising moon, drawn towards the luminous presence of starlight on the beach. His mother turned towards him, her emerald eyes wide with fear, and her mouth hung open in a gaping scream.

"Stay away."

Percy heard the harsh, distorted echo of his mother's sweet voice shouting to him. Vivid images flitted through his mind's eyes.

A monstrous wolf crept out of seclusion, its black fur matted and falling out in clumps, exposing diseased flesh underneath its mangy coat; snarling, its jaws snapped open and closed, ropes of saliva hanging from gnarled teeth. Sharpened nails jutted from its giant paws, burrowing into the earth, and ripping out chunks of soil as it pursued Percy's mother. With its back hunched high in the air, it kept its head low to the ground, using its giant nostrils to inhale and track the lavender perfume left behind by his mother.

Chased by the fearsome creature, Percy's mother ran up the stairs, dashing into the cottage across the lake. An alarm went off in Percy's head. Somehow, he realized the danger lurking within that isolated cottage was far worse than the beast hunting. Slanted towards the lake, the weathered frame appeared ready to collapse at any moment. The wolf leapt against the door, its jagged claws tearing into wood, shredding splinters from the frame; it shuddered against the beast's weight. It wouldn't be long before the determined animal made its way inside to devour his mother. But Percy sensed an evil presence awaiting her inside that cottage. Far worse than the beast outside.

"You need to get out of there!" Percy yelled, trying to warn his mother.

A deafening clap rattled the cottage: windows exploded, wood splintered and cracked, and the earth trembled. Terrified, the wolf dashed back into the woods, vanishing into the darkness. Something pounded the ground from below the grass, sending a rolling wave across the lake and onto the shore, and tufts of grass and dirt exploded upwards as the ground rolled towards Percy.

"Run."

Percy bolted upright in his bed. Coated in a layer of perspiration, the bed sheets clung to him. Dazed, Percy opened the curtains and stared out into the blackness. The moon was hidden behind a veil of clouds, a faint trace of silvery light all that remained to light the night sky in the town of Crooked Creek. A flashing red, white, and blue light caught in the trees surrounding Percy's neighborhood.

Another horrendous nightmare. Since his mother disappeared days ago, lucid dreams tormented him mercilessly. A thunderous boom rattled the front door, the rickety screen screeching from the vigorous blows. In a confused haze, Percy wandered out of his room and towards the stairs. As he passed his parents' bedroom, he saw the faint flicker of moonlight catch in an aluminum can. His stepfather Ben, passed out drunk and sprawled face-first in his bed, moaned and rolled over, the tangled sheets clumped around his body in a heap. Yellow stains marred the white blankets and the stale aroma of beer sweat poured out of the room.

"Asshole," Percy muttered as another series of rhythmic knocks rattled the door.

His feet thumped down the stairs, his head clouded and muddled by the terrible visions of his mother. Outside, the sharp static buzz of a radio snapped on. A muffled voice filtered through the door, followed by the sound of fading footsteps. Percy rushed to the door and threw it open, revealing a police officer.

The officer stopped dead in her tracks and glanced over her shoulder. "Is your father home, young man?" she asked, her voice comforting yet stern. Held in her left hand, her peaked cap concealed her holster from view.

Behind her, the flashing lights of her squad car had already drawn people to their windows, with the eyes of his neighbors peering at him from behind the curtains. Another officer sat behind the wheel, his hat resting crooked atop his head. He pushed it down so that it rested just above his eyebrows, then pushed his door open; the hinges creaked as the man lumbered out of the car.

Speechless, Percy stood in the doorway, the chilly night air sending a shiver down his spine. The officer's black work boots thudded off the stairs as he made his way up to stand beside his partner. He removed his hat and held it across his chest.

"This is the Benoit residence?"

"Y-y-yes," Percy stammered.

"Where is your dad?" He flipped open his notepad, his finger explored the page. "Ben," he continued after a lengthy pause, his voice void of any sincere emotion.

Percy stared down at his feet. "He's in bed."

"Can we come inside?" the female officer asked.

Without acknowledging her, Percy stepped aside and allowed the officers to shuffle through the door and in through the porch.

"Where?" the male officer questioned, nudging his way further into the house.

"Upstairs," Percy answered.

The female's worried gaze wandered down towards Percy's feet; she forced herself to make eye contact, placing a hand on his shoulder. "I'm Officer Petterson, and he's Officer Bugden." She pointed towards him as he made his way up the stairs, his heavy boots clomping off each step. "What's your name?"

"Percy," he replied, his voice cracking. "Did you find my mother?"

From upstairs, the sound of Ben's confused groans cut short by Officer Bugden's resounding rapport. "Get up, Mr. Benoit."

Percy stared into Petterson's eyes, his bottom lip quivering. "Just tell me, please," he begged.

Petterson sighed, her gaze shifting to the top of the stairs before finding its way back to Percy. "I'm sorry," she said, her voice trailing off.

Tears welled in the corner of his eyes and spilled out

over his cheeks. Deep, hitching sobs shook his body. He buried his face into Petterson's jacket. She pulled him close, embracing him as he mourned.

Behind Percy, fumbling footsteps lumbered down the staircase. When he turned around, he saw Officer Bugden guiding Ben down the stairs towards them with excess force. The waistband of Ben's flannel sleep pants hugged his hips, threatening to fall to the floor as he scuffled his feet in a drunken stagger.

"How did this happen?" Ben demanded, his voice haggard.

Percy stepped aside and leaned his back against the wall as Officer Bugden pushed Ben towards the door; the scent of whisky and vomit filled Percy's nostrils as he caught a whiff of Ben's body odour.

"Calm down, Mr. Benoit," Officer Bugden said with authority.

Officer Petterson stepped between Ben and Percy, shielding him from his stepfather's wrathful eyes. "Let him sleep it off in the drunk tank and we can ask him once he sobers up."

Percy appreciated her candid attempt to defuse the situation before it escalated, but he wanted answers to the questions racing through his mind.

Ben pushed Officer Bugden's hand away, twisting his upper body, and lurched towards Percy, tripping over his own feet and stumbling into the wall. Angry, Ben thrust his finger towards Percy. "If you think I did this," he said, slurring his words. But before Ben could finish his sentence, he submerged his head into his hands and a series of sobs stifled his words. Officer Bugden dragged Ben to his feet, gave Percy a nod, and dragged Ben outside.

Petterson turned back to Percy, her blonde hair framing her face. Kind blue eyes studied Percy. "How old are you?"

"I'm seventeen," Percy lied; he wouldn't turn seventeen until the end of the school year. But he hoped that would pry answers from the officer.

Petterson stared at the ceiling, shaking her head. "We found your mom's car near Crooked Feeder Bridge."

"Why would she be out there?" the question fell out of his mouth before he realized it.

"The coroner has to confirm, but it looks like she overdosed."

"There's no way!" Percy shouted, outraged. "My mom didn't use drugs."

"I'm so sorry, kid." Petterson spoke softly. "Come on, I'll take you down to the station."

Percy glared out at the squad car, finding Ben's face slumped against the window; drool running down his chin and his eyes clamped shut. "I don't want to go with him. I want my mom," Percy whispered.

"Your mother is dead," Petterson rasped, cackling.

When Percy turned to face Petterson, he watched her face slide off, the folds of skin slopping the muscle and spilling onto the floor with a wet plop. Beneath the skin, scarlet blood dripped down and over the officer's uniform, splattering on the floor. Percy stumbled backwards, tripping on the door stop, and tumbled out of the house onto the concrete steps. Not waiting for Petterson to chase him, he rolled down the steps and landed hard on the stony walkway; rocks skittered across the lawn with his landing.

Petterson lurched through the doorway, her skin molting from her body, revealing the muscle and sinew beneath in a graphic display of gore, and her jaw hung open in a lipless sneer. Blood splashed over the concrete, leaving a greasy smear behind as she dragged herself forward. Her arms and legs, working in demonic choreography, jutted and snapped into place with sickening pops.

As Percy found his way to his feet, a stiff hand fell on his shoulder like a dead weight. He spun around, expecting to find the police officer standing before him, but Ben's sneering grin greeted him. Clutched in Ben's fist, Bugden's severed head dangled aimlessly, droplets of blood casting a wide arc across the lawn.

"Jesus Christ," Percy whispered, unable to move his legs.

He was frozen in place by his stepfather's bulging eyes: tiny red rivers spread across the sclera, with the edges rimmed with yellowish-pink puss that oozed down his cheeks. Ben swung the severed head back and forth like a pendulum, gathering momentum. "Head's up, slugger," Ben guffawed, slinging Bugden's head towards Percy.

It landed against Percy's chest with a solid thump, compressing his ribcage and driving the wind from his lungs. Instinctively, Percy caught the head, his fingers entwining into a tangle of hair. Fiery red hair snaked over his knuckles and draped over his forearms. Wide-eyed, Percy stared down into the vacant stare of his mother's listless emerald eyes.

"Get out of my head!" Percy screamed, dropping the skull and blacking out.

V. Hangover

Hidden beneath the mist of dawn, steam ascended from Deadman's Lake's glossy black surface. A solitary loon called out to the rising sun, peeking out from beneath a veil of clouds, greeting the day. Tendrils of fog snaked over the stony beach, creeping towards the forest. Moisture from the lake coated everything in a thick dew while beads of water dripped from the branches, dropping to the muddied earth below.

Percy rolled over in his sleeping bag, causing the rocks to shift beneath him. Uncomfortable, he woke up. Remnants of sleep glued his eyes shut, the lashes clumped together. As he struggled to sit up, he encountered a wave of nausea washing over him. Unable to fight it, he rolled over onto his side and dry heaved. When his stomach muscles relaxed, he groaned, holding his palm to his forehead to ease his pounding headache.

The vague images from last night's nightmare were quickly becoming a distant memory, forced from his mind by the hangover dominating his entire body. Percy rolled onto his side to search for his prescription on the nightstand. His fingers fumbled over the craggy, wet beach. It took him far too long to realize that he wasn't in his room, and he let out a defeated groan.

"And yet," Damien said, his voice came from somewhere behind Percy, "he lives."

Percy grumbled incoherently with his head buried in his chest. Images of the previous night raced through his mind, blurring into a flash of colours, aggravating his headache. Only one image stood out in his mind: fiery red hair. It reminded him of a smoldering fire in winter. Red-hot embers, vibrant against January snowfall. But he couldn't remember why. Angie had jet black hair, so that couldn't be it.

"What are you saying?" Damien grinned.

Percy raised his eyes towards Damien, indebted to the clouds for dulling the sunlight. Even the faint trickle of daylight wrecked havoc on him. "I said, not so loud," he groaned. Despite the tarp overhead, water seeped up through the beach and into his sleeping bag, soaking into his jeans.

"How are you feeling today?"

"Like a truck ran over me," Percy complained. "How come you're not hungover?"

"We've all drank before," Damien said. He crouched under the tarp and shuffled towards Percy. "You'll get used to it." He held out two white caplets in one hand and a plastic bottle of water in the other.

Without bothering to ask what they were, Percy popped the pills into his mouth and chugged back the water. The caplets lodged in his parched throat, gagging him. No matter how much water he guzzled, he couldn't keep any moisture in his mouth. When the pills slid down, he belched.

"Are you still up for a little walk?"

"Do you mean right now?" Percy scratched at the back of his head, working his fingers through the tangles in his shaggy hair. "I'd rather lay down for a little while."

"Oh, come on, man," Damien pleaded. "Don't you remember last night?"

Percy laughed and instantly regretted it: everything hurt. "Actually…" Percy started.

"You promised that we'd check out the cottage. Impress the girls with how brave you've become. You don't recall at all, do you?" Damien sighed.

"Sorry, pal, I honestly don't." Percy reached his hand out to Damien for help. With no effort, his friend yanked him to his feet. He felt the contents of his stomach slosh around inside and raised his hand to cover his mouth. The urge to vomit ebbed and waned without reason.

"Dude," Damien whined, drawing the word out. "You promised Angie you'd bring her something back from inside the cabin."

Percy gulped nervously. Things were spiraling out of control, pushing the limitations of his bravery. He avoided Damien's gaze, choosing instead to stare at the rocks beneath him. Internal conflict erupted within him, peer pressure corrupting the morals his mother taught him. He was worried he'd lose another part of her, afraid that his memories would fade away if he surrendered himself down this path.

"I don't know," Percy muttered to himself.

"It's a victimless crime," Damien responded, oblivious to Percy's attempted internal soliloquy. "All we need is to take a cup or some odd trinket from that abandoned cottage, and bring it back."

"What if it belongs to somebody?"

"Who?" Damien chuckled. "No one has bothered to claim the belongings after twenty years. I think it's safe to say we have carte blanch. Besides," a grin swept across Damien's face, "Angie will think you're so brave. It's totally worth it, dude."

Percy groaned, finding himself stumbling over the rock along the beach. The stony shore stretched out into a straight line until it reached Rushing Fall River. They trudged along in silence, cutting across the river by using the makeshift bridge they built last year, which amounted to nothing more than a pile of rocks. But it kept Percy's feet clear of the frigid waters. Ahead, the shoreline cut abruptly towards the other side. From this angle, trees shrouded the cottage from view. The sound of a truck door slamming shut sent a flock of birds fluttering into the sky.

"Did you hear that?" Percy stopped dead in his tracks.

"Yeah," Damien answered. "It's just one of the older kids out for a joy ride."

"But what if it's not?"

"Like, it's the cops or something?"

"I don't think this is such a good idea anymore," Percy said, slowing his pace to a near stop.

"Don't be such a wimp," Damien snapped. He didn't wait for Percy, pushing forward.

Percy watched his friend vanish into the forest, heading down the overgrown path that would lead them directly to the cottage. He hesitated, his heart thumping in his chest to match the pounding in his head. He kicked at the rocks, sending them clattering towards the lake. They vanished into the fog before splashing in the shallow water along the edge of the craggy shore. The energetic racket of branches bending and snapping back faded away.

"Damn it," Percy sighed, heading towards the path to follow Damien. He had to duck, the branches drooping low with dew. The ground reeked of muck, decay, and overturned soil. Revolted by the stench, Percy dashed through the path, the stray branches nipping at him, tearing scratches across his arms.

He stumbled over a half-buried root, falling forwards and tumbling into the hard-packed dirt driveway. The dilapidated cabin loomed over him, the two upstairs windows peering down at him. Grey, weathered boards in desperate need of restoration gave the cottage a dreadful, haunted appearance. All the ghost stories Damien told last night threatened to come true. The back door hung open, darkness spewing from within, and its hinges squeaked and whined. It sounded as if the cottage were speaking to him, warning him to stay away. A fetid aroma wafted from some place deep within the bowels of the cottage.

"Are you alright?"

A sweet, angelic voice rose from behind him. Gentle footsteps approached, scuffing up the dirt as the stranger approached. "You took quite the tumble," the woman commented.

"I'm fine," Percy grumbled, pushing himself up from the ground into a kneeling position, resting his hands on his hips. "I tripped on a root or something."

"Do you need help?"

"No," Percy cut her off, his tone sharper than he meant

for it to be. He struggled to get to his feet, scrubbing the dirt off his jeans and shirt. "Really, I'm fine. Thank you."

Too flustered to turn around, he sauntered towards the cottage. When he found himself within the looming shadow, a chill raced down his spine.

"Excuse me," the girl called out. "And where do you think you're going?" Her shoes thundered down the driveway towards him.

Percy paused, shuffling his feet in place. It took a moment before the puzzle pieces clicked into place. The truck in the driveway, the door wide open.

"Is this your cabin?"

"It's my father's," the girl answered, standing so close behind him he could sense her breath on his neck. Goosebumps riddled his flesh.

He spun around and froze, gawking at the girl before him. Fiery locks of hair silhouetted her face. Her piercing sea-foam eyes captured his attention, drawing his gaze. She smiled, her ruby red lips dull compared to her glistening, red mane. Freckles coated her creamy complexion, the brownish-red dots littering her cheeks. Dressed in an unbuttoned blue plaid shirt that billowed in the breeze, and a grey tee, with the words *Memorial University* in bold block letters, tucked into short denim jeans, she looked ready to head to college. She held a moving box against her stomach with firm hands. Captivated by the girl's familiar beauty, Percy stared at her, unable to take his eyes away from her. He stood there with his jaw gaping open.

The girl shifted on her feet under his gaze, off put by Percy's wandering eye. "Kiddo," she started. "Are you sure you're okay?"

Only one person in the world called him *kiddo*, and this young girl happened to be the spitting image of her. It couldn't be true. But somehow, he knew it had to be.

"Mom," Percy exhaled, releasing his breath that he hadn't realized he'd been holding. Overwhelmed, the world spun out of control around him. Green blurred into drab grey as he collapsed onto his backside. "Mom," he sputtered as he drifted towards oblivion again...

...That familiar voice lulling him to sleep once more.

VI. New to Town

A jumble of voices bored into Percy's skull. His vision fragmented and blurred, struggling to focus. Beside him, something smooth pressed against his arm. When his vision focused, the red-headed girl hovered over him. His mother's eyes gazed upon him, but it couldn't be his mom. She was far too young; the woman before him seemed created from memories ripped from his childhood, from days spent home from school with his mother tending to him at his bedside when he had been five.

"Mom?" he mumbled, scratching at the back of his head. His fingers discovered a wet spot and probed it. Percy stared at the tips of his fingers. Painted red with watery blood, he returned his hand to the superficial wound. The dew from the ground dampened his hair, mixing with the blood; when he looked at his hand again, only a faint trace of red remained.

A serene smile stretched across the girl's face as she shook her head. But she didn't respond.

"Christ, Percy," Damien said. "You must have hit your head hard." He gestured towards the young woman. "I'm sorry about my friend," he continued, then leaned in close and whispered in Percy's ear. "You're embarrassing yourself, dude. Stop calling her mom, please."

Ignoring Damien, Percy stared at his mother's doppelgänger. "You look just like my mother. When she was younger," he added.

The young woman rose with her eyes lingering on Percy, an awkward smile plastered on her face. "I guess he'll be okay, Dad," she announced.

A man strode into view. His salt and pepper hair gave him a distinguished dignity. "You gave us a good scare, kid," he declared, his voice brusque. He towered over his daughter, resting his hand on her shoulder. Tucked beneath his arm, the red cross of the first aid kit stood out in sharp contrast to the white container. A gold chain shimmering with the faint daylight dangled around his neck.

Damien helped Percy to his feet. The four of them stood in the driveway, the sun breaking through the clouds overhead. Unable to shake the old memories of his mother that this girl brought to the surface, Percy shuffled his feet back and forth. He searched for something to say, anything to break the silence. But he stood there with his jaw hanging open and his hands in his pockets. He detected an unwanted glare from the father, almost challenging Percy.

"What's your name, kiddo?" the girl asked, using his mother's familiar phrase.

Surprised once more, Percy struggled to find his breath. The world closed in on him again. A ray of sunshine caught in her tangles, inflaming her hair; it glowed with fevered intensity. Her smile faltered, a nervous grimace taking its place.

"His name is Percy," Damien spoke up. "And I'm

Damien."

"It's nice to meet you, Percy," the girl said, holding out her hand.

Percy rubbed his hands against his jeans, trying to dry the sweat off his palms. Hesitantly, he reached out and clasped her hand. Her touch ignited a spark inside of him. Confused, he stepped back, staring down at his feet. While his mind raced with questions and possibilities, the girl spoke with Damien. Their words were a distant murmur in his muddled mind. One thing stood out, drawing his attention. "What did you say your name was?"

"Mary Lee," she replied.

"That was my mother's name," Percy whispered. He spotted a faint glimmer of rosy colour flush on her cheeks and her eyes narrowed, concentrating on him. Creases formed along her forehead and across the bridge of her nose. And for a moment, she aged into a mirror image of his mother; his heart skipped a beat.

"Strange," Damien said, shattering the painful silence.

"If you don't mind," the father started, then paused. "We have a long day of unpacking ahead of us, and we should get to it." His hand guided his daughter away from the boys.

"Wait," Percy said, raising his voice.

The father turned around, a vexed expression painting his face. Mary Lee kept walking towards the truck, her hair bobbed against her shoulders.

"We want to help," Percy declared, his voice wavering.

"What?" Damien said, stunned by Percy's offer.

"If you need a hand, we'd be glad to help. Wouldn't we, Damien?"

"Uh, sure," Damien reluctantly agreed. "That sounds like fun," he added, his tone heavy with sarcasm.

"I guess I could use a hand," the father admitted. "Once we unload the truck, we need to haul all that old crap out and make a trip to the dump. Plus, we need to run back into town to pick up some groceries for tonight. And sooner would be better than later." Without another word, the father turned and walked towards his truck.

Mary Lee passed him, carrying a brown cardboard box, the word *kitchen* scrawled in black marker across it. She winked at Percy, his mother's smile on her face. The stairs groaned as she headed into the cottage, vanishing into the dim light.

When they were alone, Damien grasped Percy by the wrist. "What are we doing here?" he snapped, working to keep his voice low but failing.

"Aren't you the one who said we need to bring back a trinket from inside for the girls?"

Damien glared at Percy, remaining silent.

"We help them, snatch something from inside, and then bring it back to the girls. It's what you wanted to do, right?"

"Okay," Damien sighed.

Percy left his friend behind and headed towards the truck. The father passed by with three boxes cradled in his arms, his face hidden behind the top box. When Percy reached the pan of the truck, he stretched out for the nearest box, sliding it across the bed and into his chest. He twisted it around until he found the scribbled black marker, showing that it belonged in the kitchen. Every muscle in his body ached, his muscles fatigued by the hangover. But he pushed the pain out of his mind and hoisted the box into his arms. He staggered toward over the driveway towards the cottage, hugging the box to his chest. Gravel crunched beneath his feet.

When he reached the stairs, a shudder raced through him. The door hung open, daring him to step into the darkness. Mary Lee and her father were inside, but he couldn't hear them anywhere. The blackness loomed before him, reaching out for him. He closed his eyes and stepped forward, the stairs swaying beneath him. Wood creaked and shrieked at him in a final warning. His heart galloped in his chest, beating off his ribcage. Something didn't feel right.

Before he could drop the box on the porch and run away, Damien nudged him up the stairs. "Let's get this over with," he complained.

Forced up the stairs, Percy stepped into the cabin. A faint trickle of light from a window shined in, catching in the dust drifting through the air. He found himself in the kitchen. The cupboards were barren and exposed. If there had been doors on them, they were long gone. A blanket of dust veiled the colour of the counters and floor, casting everything in a dingy shade of grey. Tucked away in the corner, a rusted-out fridge took up space. A burned-out stove sat in the midst of the counter, cutting it into two equal halves; the door hung crooked off the hinge, one edge resting on the floor below.

The stagnant air filled his lungs, and for a moment, he didn't think he could survive inside. A breeze whispered in his ears, imploring him to leave this place.

"It stinks in here," Damien said, pushing past his friend. "Rat feces and decay. These people have a ton of work ahead of them."

"Where are they?"

Panic settled in. Percy needed to get out of this cottage. He abandoned his box on the counter. A puff of dust exploded into the air. Left behind on the windowsill, a figurine coated in grime and mold called out to him. He snatched it, crammed it into his pocket, and bolted down the stairs.

Damien followed behind. "Wait up!" he called out.

"I thought you wanted to help?" Mary Lee's father called out after them from within the darkness of the cottage.

Percy stopped dead in his tracks. "I'm sorry, I forgot I have baseball practice," he lied.

Without saying another word, the boys left and ducked into the woods. The canopy overhead blocked out the sun, casting them in long shadows. Percy refused to stop trudging through the woods until they reached the other side. When they burst onto the beach, with the cottage hidden behind the trees, Percy breathed a sigh of relief.

"You think Angie's going to want that figurine you stole?"

Percy dug it out of his pocket and wandered down to the beach. He submerged the glass figure into Deadman's Lake and scrubbed the grime off, exposing the flaming red hair from beneath the layers of dirt.

"What is going on?" Percy muttered to himself, concealing his increasing dread. A sweet voice rises with the wind, whispering a beautiful haiku in his ear, turning his thoughts towards Angie, stuffing the figurine deep in his pocket.

"Smoldering embers,

"Burning with intense desire,

"Passionately kiss..."

"What are you thinking about?" Damien asked with a sly grin. "You have a crush on her, don't you?"

"Shut up," Percy laughed. "Jerk."

VII. Standing Tall

Percy trudged down his street, with his head hung low, going through the motions. He passed his stepfather's truck, his finger tracing the rusted panel. He wasn't worrying about what Ben would say when he strolled into the house on drunken legs; he was no longer afraid of Ben's temper. He had bigger concerns to worry about. He couldn't stop thinking about the strange vibe he sensed inside the cottage. Something about the figurine in his back pocket bothered him. And he couldn't cease thinking about his mother; that tormented him the most.

The screen door creaked, and he discovered the front door unlocked. When he stepped inside, the screen door slammed closed, startling him. A stale reek of beer assaulted his nostrils, a harrowing reminder of the night before. Still hungover, he fought the urge to vomit. The television blared Morgan Freeman's voice from the living room. Percy poked his head around the corner, finding Ben slouched in his armchair, a beer can clutched in his grasp.

"Where did you run off to last night?" he slurred his words; a pile of crushed aluminum beer cans lay defeated around the recliner.

Percy hesitated. "I went camping at Deadman's Lake with my friends."

Ben leaned forward, and the worn out springs groaned under his weight. "Is that so?" he grunted.

"Yeah," Percy answered, turning away from Ben and opening the fridge. Aluminum cans crumpled behind him as Ben staggered to his feet. "I'm just home long enough to grab something to eat and head back out," he said, making sure his tone remained steady.

Ben stumbled into the kitchen and belched. His rancid breath wafted over Percy's shoulder, the stench turning his stomach. He raised his hand, covering his mouth with his palm, fighting the rising bile eating away at the back of his throat. The appalling stench lingered, permeating the crisp air of the fridge. Percy took a jar of strawberry jam and a jug of milk and let the door slam shut as he strode to the counter, avoiding eye contact with Ben.

"What's the matter, boy?" Ben spat out the question as if it were venom in his mouth. "Too afraid to look at me now?" he roared.

Percy opened the cupboards, fetched the peanut butter, and got himself a knife from the drawer, keeping his back turned to his stepfather. Then he poured himself a glass of milk, draining half of it in one mouthful, refilled his cup, then placed the jug back in the fridge. A blast of glacial air poured from the fridge, causing the hairs on his arm to stand up straight.

"Cat got your tongue?" Ben laid his hand on Percy's shoulder, wrenching him around. A spiteful snarl bared his yellowed teeth.

"Are you going to hit me?" Percy stood his ground.

Ben let Percy go, his eyes wild with anger, a snarl cast wrinkles across his face. His mouth hung open in silent incredulity.

"I didn't think so," Percy said, squaring his shoulders to Ben, discovering his courage. Inside, his heart thrashed against his ribcage. He didn't know what to expect from Ben. Once the initial shock wore off, he may snap. But Percy refused to withdraw now. Tensing up, he braced himself for whatever awaited him.

"Don't you talk to me like that," Ben snapped, taking a step backwards.

Percy relaxed, releasing his breath he hadn't realized he'd been holding. He returned to making his sandwich, slathering one slice of bread with a healthy portion of peanut butter, and the other with a thick layer of jam. He took a bite; globs of strawberry goo dribbled over his chin and the peanut butter fixed to the roof of his mouth.

Ben ducked into the fridge, rummaging through the shelves, cursing under his breath. The hiss of carbonation rang out, and when Ben stood up, a sullen frown pressed his lips against his teeth. He guzzled a mouthful of beer. Suds ran down from the corner of his lips, and he wiped his face with the back of his hand.

"Have you been looking for a job?" Ben spoke in between gulps of beer. "Like we've discussed," he added.

"No," Percy answered. "Not yet."

Ben glared at him, swaying on unsteady feet. "Don't be asking me for money. You are big and ugly enough to make your own."

Percy took a bite out of his sandwich, chewing it with his mouth open. "Will you put this on my tab? Or do I need to pay now?"

"Don't push it," Ben said, raising his voice and thrusting a finger towards Percy. For a moment, the tension in the room grew thick, making it hard to move. "And you're going to need to pitch in around here, or else."

"Or else?"

Without saying a word, Ben turned and wandered back to his recliner, plunking himself down into his chair. He took another slug of beer, then he drooped his arm over the side of the recliner. The beer sloshed around inside the can. "Before you leave, do the dishes and take out the trash on your way out," he demanded.

Percy ran the water, grumbling under his breath. Luckily for him, Ben's diet comprised a steady intake of liquid lunch and canned ravioli. There were no filthy dishes for him to wash, and it wasn't worth arguing with Ben over this meaningless chore. It would take him less than five minutes. Another fight could last hours, and he didn't want to keep Angie waiting at the tree house.

Percy added dish liquid, and bubbles, stained red by tomato sauce, grew into a mushroom cloud, rising from the surface of the steamy water. The glass bowls clunked off the side of the sink as he dug around the bottom for his glass; he washed it first, just like his mother always had. Next, he scrubbed the bowls and utensils, heaping them into the drying rack to air dry. Then he drained the sink. The roar of imbibing water drew Ben's attention. He twisted his neck, peering at Percy over the top of his recliner.

"See," Ben called out over his movie. "That wasn't so hard, was it?"

Percy searched beneath the sink cupboard, finding a blue recycle bag. He took it with him into the living room, picking up the beer cans from the floor. "You know there's a garbage can in the kitchen, right?"

"Just do as you're told," Ben mumbled, keeping his eyes glued to the television.

On the screen, the camera panned over the Shawshank prison yard. Despite his love for this movie, he finished picking up the cans and headed back into the kitchen. He emptied the rest of the recyclables into the bag, hauled the garbage out of the bin, and slipped his shoes on. His lungs thanked him for the breath of fresh air, and he wandered to the end of the driveway, taking deep breaths. He tossed the garbage into the bins in the front yard and looked back at his childhood home.

"My Shawshank," he muttered to himself.

The screen door hung half off its hinges, concealing the drab beige door. Dangling with gravity, the still shiny doorknob hung at a crooked angle. Tangles of weeds sprung from the cracks in the walkway, splitting the asphalt. Overgrown grass, scorched by the sun, lay across the lawn in heaps of yellow. Slanted towards the driveway, the steps appeared to lean away from the house. Sunlight died on the water-stained windows. Percy's eyes wandered to his bedroom window. Hidden behind black, drawn curtains, his childhood memories were lost deep within the gloom.

Before he could leave, he had to pack his sleeping bag and change of clothes. Filled with a sense of dread, he took a deep breath and headed back inside. He passed Ben without a word and clambered up the stairs, feeling them swaying beneath him. Cast in darkness, his bedroom dared him to enter, monsters hiding in the shadows. He flicked on his light, the dull yellow glow losing its battle with the darkness.

Percy flung open his curtains, allowing daylight to trickle in, vanquishing the long shadows in his room. He pulled out his sleeping bag, stuffing it into his backpack, and crammed in a change of clothes for tomorrow. Before he forgot, he took the glass figurine from the cottage out of his pocket, wrapped it in a paper towel, and tucked it into his sleeping bag. Then he checked his watch, realizing if he didn't hurry, Angie would think he stood her up. He opened up his closet and reached on the top shelf, pulling down a small wooden box. With no time to search through it, he stuffed it into a side pouch, then raced down the stairs.

Slumped in the chair, Ben's head lolled to the side as he snored, his jaw hanging wide open. Percy stared down at Ben, dark thoughts and hatred clouding his mind, his hands balled into tight fists. Something jabbed his wrist, and a sharp pain radiated from it. For a moment, he blacked out. And when he opened his eyes, he stood in front of the sink. Immediately drawing his attention, the knife, smothered in crimson globs of strawberry jam staining the counter, lay just out of reach.

Behind him, Ben had fallen into a deep, soundless sleep; his right arm dangled over the armrest, his fingers outstretched for his last can of beer. He didn't want to risk waking Ben up; but he couldn't walk away from the last dish. Ben would lose his mind at him for being lazy. Percy ran the hot water, running over the blade and dripping into the sink, stained scarlet red. He grabbed a dishtowel and wiped down the counter, then left through the back door, letting the screen door slam shut against its frame, no longer caring if he woke Ben up or not.

Nestled at the end of a cul-de-sac, Damien's home perched on a pristinely cut terrace. The hedges were all neatly pruned, and a tire swing hung from an enormous oak tree along the side of the house. Large windows greeted the rays of sunlight, reflecting the light back at Percy. Embraced by the enveloping nature, ivy climbed the red bricked exterior, spreading towards the roof. Black asphalt stretched along the far side of the house, leading towards a two-car garage attached to the house. Left open, the double door showed off fancy toys inside; the grill of the Mercedes Benz shimmered in the daylight.

A welcoming porch stretched across the entire front, with pillars that reached up to the awning. Between two rocking chairs, a table rested below the window. A radio rested on the table alongside an ash tray. On the other side, a long outdoor couch and three single chairs were arranged around an oval table.

Percy rapped his knuckles off Damien's door. Inside, he could hear Damien's mother call out for him to answer the door. Damien's footsteps thundered down the stairs, and the door flew open.

"You made it," Damien said, stepping aside to let his friend in.

"Is that Percy?" Damien's mother called out from the living room.

"Yes, Mom," Damien answered, almost snapping.

"Send him in here."

Damien rolled his eyes and sighed. "Listen," Damien started. "Before you talk to her, there's something you should know. I just don't want you to be mad at me, okay?"

Percy crossed his arm across his chest, shaking his head. He waited impatiently for Damien to spill his guts, glaring at his friend.

"I told her you should stay here for a few days." Damien paused, his eyes studying Percy. "You know, because of your dad."

Without saying a word, Percy pushed past his friend and headed into the Colbourne's living room. He found her rocking in her plush leather recliner, holding a drink in her hand, taking a sip as Percy walked into the room. The lush carpet felt wonderful against his feet, soothing his tired feet; he hadn't realized how far he had walked over the last twenty-four hours.

"Hi, Mrs. Colbourne," Percy said, waving his hand and regretting it.

"Have a seat, young man," she replied, her voice soft but authoritative. "And please, call me Betty."

Percy made his way to the elegant leather couch and sank heavily into the cushions. If this had been under different circumstances, he would have fallen into a deep sleep. Instead, he forced himself to sit up straight. The air conditioner blasted glacial air into the room.

Betty placed her drink on the table beside her; the ice clanked against the side of the glass. "Now, Percy, I will not beat around the bush here. Damien told me about you and your stepdad, and that you may want to spend a few nights here."

Stunned by her bluntness, Percy entwined his fingers, fidgeting nervously.

"You're a big boy now," she continued, not giving Percy time to chime in. "All I will say is that if you ever need anything, our door is always open."

"Thanks, Mrs. Colbourne."

"Mrs. Colbourne makes me sound ancient, Percy. Please, call me Betty," she laughed.

"Will do," Percy smiled. "Betty."

"Are you staying for supper, Percy?"

"Not tonight. I'm meeting someone, and I'd be late if I stuck around," Percy explained.

"Perhaps tomorrow," Betty suggested, smiling back at Percy.

"That would be nice." Percy stood up from the couch, wishing he could stay a little longer; but would Angie wait for him?

Percy wandered into the kitchen. Every appliance in the kitchen glimmered, the bountiful sunlight captured by the stainless steel. The tiled floor glistened with a single, stretched out yellow ray that cut the room in half. Damien sat at the kitchen table, a guilty expression adding weight to his face. A glass of soda pop rested on the table, the bubbles fizzing and dancing amongst the ice cubes.

Pulling out a chair, Percy sat across from his friend, who refused to meet his gaze. For a moment, their eyes locked; both boys remained silent. Percy unslung his bookbag and dropped it to the floor beside him; the sleeping bag absorbed the shock of the fall. Damien had broken an unwritten rule. But Percy couldn't stay mad. "Is there any more in the fridge?" Percy pointed at the glass.

Damien nodded, got up, and poked his head into the fridge. When the door opened, Percy couldn't help notice the colourful cornucopia of food crammed inside. Citrus fruits, vibrant vegetables, and brightly packaged food filled every shelf. The sight of all that food made Percy both jealous and ravenous. His stomach growled.

"Can you grab me something from the fridge?"

Taken aback, Damien paused with the fridge door wide open. He stared at Percy with wide eyes. "You've never asked for anything to eat before. What do you like?" he chuckled.

"It doesn't matter," Percy answered. "Anything that I can take with me; I don't want to stand Angie up."

Damien buried his head in the fridge, moving things around on the shelves. "Here we go," he exclaimed, tossing a chocolate bar at Percy. When he stood up, he held a container of raspberries and a can of coke and placed them on the table. He opened the container, the plastic crinkled and popped as he struggled with the packaging.

"Thanks," Percy said, opening his soda and taking a gulp, enjoying the carbonation on his tongue. He held the red can in front of him and tried to remember the last time he had a brand name soda pop.

"So, what's your plan with Angie?"

"What do you mean? I don't have a plan. Should I have one?" Percy leaned across the table, grabbing a handful of the bright red berries; they were both sweet and tart.

Damien laughed. A sly grin creased his cheeks. "Well, I put in a friendly word for you with her."

"When did you speak to her?"

"After I got home, I called her," Damien replied.

"Why do you have her number?" Percy felt jealousy creeping through his system, and his face burned red.

"We've been friends since junior high," he explained. "Not all of us are afraid to speak to a girl."

"Whatever," Percy mumbled, gulping down his soda. He let out a belch in between drinks, finishing the can off without putting it down. "Anyway," Percy grunted, pushing his chair away from the table, "I should get going before Angie thinks I stood her up. Are you coming to the tree house tonight?"

"Isn't that for children?" Damien sighed. "The last time we went, weren't we ten?"

"I got us into that cottage," Percy started. "I'm just asking you to stay with me tonight."

"Why are you so obsessed with those people moving into that cottage?"

Percy grabbed his bookbag, unzipped the side pouch, and placed the wooden box on the table between them. He slipped the top off, the wooden top scratching along the groove. Percy pulled out a stack of photos, thumbing through them. "Here we go," he said, slapping a photograph on the table.

Damien stared at it, his eyes wide with bewilderment.

"That's a picture I found of my mom from her days at university." He held up the photo so that Damien could get a better look at it.

"That's the girl," Damien stammered in disbelief. "From the cottage."

"Something strange is happening here," Percy said, rooting through the box. His mother's class ring should be in here. A frantic panic quickened his fingers, rattling the contents of the box off the sides.

"Why do you have a picture of that girl?"

In the distance, a branch snapped. Birds called back and forth to each other, fluttering between the trees. Both boys stared out the window, at the fleeing birds silhouetted against the horizon. Footfalls approached, scuffing through the pine needles on the trail leading towards the back patio. Elongated shadows crept across the shed, lurking just out of sight, moving swiftly towards them.

Damien's father walked past the window, pushing a wheelbarrow full of dirt with tools littered on top. He pulled a blue handkerchief from his back pocket and wiped the sweat from his forehead. Clearly out of his element, the doctor's shoulders slumped with the burden of yard work.

"Percy, why do you have a picture of that girl?" Damien said, shattering the silence.

"That's my mom," Percy repeated himself, his tone more insistent. "You don't believe me?" He didn't need a verbal response; Damien's expression betrayed him.

Damien chuckled. "Maybe it's time for you to get some help."

Percy pushed his chair backwards, tipping it over; the wooden back clapped off the tiled floor. Furious, Percy stormed out of the kitchen and gathered his shoes in his hand.

"Percy," Betty called out as Percy slammed the door shut behind him.

Percy climbed his way up to the weathered treehouse by the rickety boards nailed into the tree. They shifted beneath his weight; the nails groaning as they lost their grip on the ancient oak. Every creaking noise sent his heart galloping, the beats blending together into a singular note. Before each step, he glanced over his shoulder: the ground appeared further away than his legs told him. With sweaty palms, he reached above him, exploring the dusty floor with his bare palm. Slivers of wood threatened to pierce his skin as he tossed his bookbag over first, then hauled himself up and over the edge.

"I thought you were brave?" Angie said, a sly smile across her face. Her tongue ran over her lips; her lipstick was a vivid shade of maroon. When she leaned forward, her tank top hung loosely from her shoulders. She followed his gaze and leaned back, crossing her arms across her chest. Embarrassed, her checks turned rosy. But her smile persisted.

Percy picked himself up, brushed himself off, and tried to hide his heavy breathing. The dying sunlight captured in her hair, accentuating the strawberry blonde strands that strayed from her face. Their eyes found each other, and Percy found himself lost in an ocean of the richest emerald waters. His jaw opened wide, and a hushed moan escaped. And his face flushed red.

Angie swayed her hips, her skirt billowing in the wind passing through the window. "Show me," she said, unable to control her excitement any longer.

Percy grabbed his bookbag, dragged it across the floor towards him, and unzipped it. Crammed inside, wrapped in a paper towel, the trinket rested in the folds of his sleeping bag. When he unwrapped Angie's prize, the figurine gave off a faint, devilish red glare as it captured the bleeding sun, illuminating the figure's hair.

"Here," Percy said, holding out the figurine for Angie.

She reached out, her fingers tracing the palm of Percy's hand, sending a wave of goosebumps up his arm. Holding it in front of her, admiring it, her eyes examined the glass figurine with great interest. First, she held it up to the light, mesmerized by the way the hair smouldered in the daylight. Then she held below her waist, the luminescent glow lingering in the glass; a thousand burning ambers running fluttering beneath the gleaming surface.

"I cleaned it up for you," Percy stammered, tripping over his words. His mouth was suddenly dry; he ran his tongue along the roof of his mouth. "What do you think?"

"It's beautiful," she claimed. Her fingers explored the contours of the figurine, tracing the hairline until the sunlight faded from the surface. "How does it do that?"

"I don't know. I've seen nothing like it before." Percy hesitated. "But it's amazing," he added.

"So," Angie started, drawing out the word before continuing. "Was it spooky inside the cabin?"

"Nah," Percy lied, unable to make eye contact with Angie. He stared out the window at the blazing orange dusk.

"Damien said you were brave." Angie took a step forward.

"Really?" Percy blushed.

She reached out and took his hand, demanding his attention. "That's what he said."

"Did he say anything else?" Percy inquired, his mind racing.

Angie shook her head. Her hair tumbled over her face, and she swept it back, tucking it behind her ear. "You sound surprised. Is there anything else you wanted to tell me?" As she stepped closer, her breath on the nape of his neck sent a wave of excitement through him.

Percy gathered his courage, inched forward into an awkward embrace, his stomach pressed against hers. He closed his eyes and leaned forward. In that moment when their lips meet, Percy feels an ever-bright flame ignite within. It lasted for an eternity within him. Time stood still, waiting for the blaze to extinguish. He felt vulnerable with a million jumbled thoughts condensed into a singular moment in time. She pulled back first; his lips parted in a breathless exhale.

When Percy opened his eyes, the sky was aflame with reds and pinks, fighting back the lurking darkness. Angie's head turned away from him, her hips twisting towards the ladder. "Did I do something wrong?" he asked.

"Do you hear that?"

The hot summer winds whispered in Percy's ear, the familiar voice warning him to run away. A creaking groan sent vibrations racing through the tree house floor. Angie stepped back, her shoulder side by side with Percy, and her hand darted down and grasped his.

"Damien?" Percy called out to the intruder. "Is that you?"

Tangles of crimson hair emerged from below. Percy's heart leapt into his chest. Startled, he stepped backwards, yanking at Angie's hand.

"Hi," Mary Lee said. Her elbows propped on the floor, her eyes taking in the situation. A smile brightened her

face. "I'm sorry," she laughed. "Am I interrupting anything?" Her smile shifted into a sly grin, her top teeth biting at her bottom lip.

"Hi," Percy responded, puzzled.

"Do you know this girl?" Angie shifted her gaze to
Percy.

"We met today," Mary Lee answered for him, pulling
herself into the tree house. The boards remained silent beneath her fragile frame. "My name's Mary Lee." She held
out her hand for Angie.

Tentatively, Angie reciprocated the gesture, her eyes
wide with adoration of the beautiful woman in front of
her. "Angie," she said. "Are you new to town?"

"My dad bought the cottage on the far side of the lake,
and we've been getting settled in," Mary Lee said.

Angie tilts her head towards Percy. "How long have
you been there?" With nimble hands, she tucked the glass
figurine into her back pocket.

"Oh, we've been staying at the Crooked Creek Inn
since last week," Mary Lee answered. "We only got the
keys today. Percy helped us move some of our stuff in
before he took off on us." She laughed.

"Do you still need help?" Percy interjected.

"No thanks. We got all the boxes inside now. All that's
left to do is the unpacking," Mary Lee said. "But that can
wait," she added.

Angie's phone buzzed, drawing her attention, the dull
glow of the screen visible in the vanishing daylight. "I better get home," she said, frowning. "My dad's wondering
why I'm back at the lake when all of my friends are at the
movies."

"I can walk you to the road," Mary Lee offered before Percy could. "It's on my way home and I'm getting tired, anyway."

"Sure," Angie agreed, her smile returning.

"Will I see you tomorrow?" Percy said, gazing at Angie with a wandering eye.

Angie leaned towards Percy, planting a delicate kiss on his cheek. "Yes," she said without a doubt, finding Percy's hands and giving them a gentle squeeze. "But I should get going now." She let go and turned towards the ladder, stopping in front of Mary Lee. "Can I get your number? Maybe we could hang out tomorrow."

"Of course," Mary Lee said with enthusiasm. "Give me your phone." Without hesitating, Angie handed over her phone. The moon hung low in the sky, casting a silvery glow over Deadman's Lake, silhouetting the girls. Mary Lee handed Angie back her phone. They hugged like old friends, pulling into a tight embrace.

"I'll see you tomorrow, Percy," Angie said, a shy smile brightening her face against the dusky sky. And then she headed down the ladder, disappearing from view.

An eerie tingle raced down Percy's spine. A crisp wind cut through the window, chilling him to the bone. Mary Lee grinned at him. The glass figurine was nestled in her palm. Embers burned within the glass figure, casting an ominous glow throughout the tree house. Her fist closed over the glass. An intense sizzling hiss filled the room; the stench of sulfur hung in the air. "I'll see you tomorrow too, kiddo," Mary Lee cackled.

Before Percy could say anything, Mary Lee slid over the edge, following Angie out of the tree house, looking down at her feet to help guide herself. Before she vanished from view, she tilted her head back up. Her smile twisted into a diabolical grin, baring her teeth at Percy with sinister intent. Black fluids flow into her pupils, turning them into two drops of oil floating across her sea foam irises, tainting the beauty of his mother's eyes.

Percy's jaw opened in a silent scream, his heart frozen in place. Mary Lee disappears, but the girls talk amongst themselves until their chatter fades, enveloped by the darkness settling over Crooked Creek, Deadman's Lake, a blackened mirror. Brought on by the blackness, the temperature plummeted; his breath hung in front of his face. A desire to protect Angie rose up inside him, but fear seized him in place.

VIII. Nightmare

Darkness enfolded Percy, with tendrils of smoky shadows closing in on him all around; his mouth hung open in a silent scream. Hanging low in the sky, a pregnant yellow moon struggled to climb into its proper place; it should have been casting its light over the forest. But an omnipresent blackness held council over Crooked Creek. A vicious wind howled through the treehouse, carrying sinister whispers to Percy from all angles, lashing out at him; the ancient oak groaned in protest, swaying towards the ground, bracing to spit Percy out. He struggled to break fear's dominance over him, straining against the unseen forces holding him in place; and begged to a God he didn't believe in for help.

A shrill creaking noise shattered the frightening trance; his leg muscles had filled with lactic acid from being tensed and strained for so long, and he stumbled to his knees, his hands darting out to break his fall. Forced to crawl on his hands and knees by exhaustion, he scrambled towards the ladder while struggling to catch his breath. He peered over the ledge into the darkness, shuddering with dread.

The ground had vanished beneath an impenetrable

blanket of black: somehow the treehouse jutted up from within the gloom. Somewhere, concealed within the shadows, Angie cried out for help. Forced to push back against the fear, Percy swung his legs over the edge, his feet searching for the first rung. As his foot found purchase on the top step, a terrified shriek startled him, throwing him off balance. His fingernails dug into the wood, tearing back at the quick as he lurched backwards towards the blackness, and blood seeped out from beneath his nails. Panicked, his arms flailed through the air as he plunged. Somehow, his hands entangled in the boards, and his body slammed hard against the tree, banging his knee off the steps. A jolt of pain raced up his leg and stars danced in his vision. Tears tracked down his cheek, and he clutched the tree, trying to reclaim his breath.

Terrified to peer over his shoulder, his foot dipped down tentatively, searching for the ground. A wave of relief eased his fluttering heart as his sneaker brushed against the ground. "Angie!" Percy called out as he dropped to the ground.

The wind drove away a muffled, cackling fit of laughter: at first, it sounded like his mother's, but it grew deeper, filtered through a phlegmy throat. Despite his growing fears and better judgement, Percy found himself drawn towards the cottage. Without thinking, he trudged through the dense foliage of the forest, not following any trail, headed in a straight line. He clambered over moss-covered rocks and ducked under fallen trees; around him, the forest reeked of sodden earth and decay.

Suddenly, Percy felt a vibration on his leg, stopping him dead in his tracks; his heart leapt into his throat, choking him. The vibration intensified. A dull buzz rang out as the forest fell silent. "Christ!" Percy cried out, pulling his cell phone out of his pocket.

"W-what the hell?" he stammered, not believing what he saw. He read the text from an unknown number in his head repeatedly — it horrified him beyond anything he could have imagined, sending a chill down his spine.

"Stay away, and don't make eye contact with the skin-walker, kiddo," his mother spoke to him, her voice stained by fear and misery.

"Skin-walker," he cursed, confused. Not understanding the warning, he dashed into the darkness, racing to Angie's aid. Tree branches lashed out at him, slashing at his face as he ran blindly through the forest. He stubbed his toes into fallen tree branches and craggy rocks, but he refused to be defeated. Determined, he made his way to the cottage.

It stood before him, desolate, leaning with the wind. Darkness filled the cottage, and the windows oozed pure blackness that devoured the interior.

"Angie!" Percy screamed his throat raw.

"Run away, kiddo," his mother's voice whispered in the wind.

"Mom!" Percy cried, glaring at the cottage.

A dismal silence settled over the forest.

Lub-dub… lub-dub… lub-dub

At first, Percy thought he heard his own heart, but it couldn't be. It belonged to someone else, something else. It must have, because the sound rumbled from beneath the ground, sending tremors through the earth. The melodic beat throbbed and pulsed, growing with anticipation.

Lub-dub-lub-dub-lub—

"Percy!" Angie's desperate plea came from within the cottage; horrified screams filled the night air.

Drawn by the sound of Angie's voice, Percy pushed his fears aside and sprinted towards the front door. The damp earth sucked Percy's feet deep into the soil, eating at him. He called out Angie's name, begging her to hold on. A raspy shriek answered him, the voice familiar but tainted with malice.

Just as he reached the steps of the cottage, a thunderous boom rattled from inside, tossing him backwards; he landed hard on his backside in the driveway, the blow forcing the air from his lungs. Shards of glass sprayed outwards as the windows shattered, raining down over him. Huddled on the ground, with his knees tucked into his chest, he covered the top of his head with both forearms and squeezed his eyes shut, protecting himself from the jagged precipitation raining down on him. Slivers of glass sliced into the flesh of his forearms and tore at his clothing, shredding the fabric.

A low, throbbing hum pulsated through the air, becoming part of Percy. His heart beat in sync with the dreadful cadence. When he opened his eyes, a pair of sinister red eyes lurked inside the darkness of the cottage, gawking at him through the open door. The creature stalked Percy, inching closer towards the edge of blackness. A guttural, choked growl accompanied the animal with every movement.

Concealed within the blackness, an anguished cry rang out, calling to Percy for help: Angie's terrified voice. Percy forced himself to his feet, groaning as he pushed through the tremendous pain. Confronted by the diabolical red eyes, Percy froze, unable to move, Percy found himself at the mercy of the vile demon lurching towards him.

"Run for your life, Percy," his mother sobbed. *"If it catches you, it will haunt you for the rest of your life until it takes what it wants from you. Why did you have to meddle in the skin-walker's business?"*

"Mom?" Percy's jaw dropped, the word tumbling out of his mouth.

Suddenly, emerging from the shadows, the demonic aberration bared its cannibal filed teeth at Percy. Reddened eyes glared at Percy, glowing with feverish intensity. Tendrils of brownish-yellow saliva hung from its bloodied jaws in thick ropes, and a rancid stench of rotten meat billowed from its stomach. Oily smoke wafted from the creature's soiled silver fur: heavy as fog, it cascaded around the beast's paws

Percy turned to run, but the ground turned to quicksand. A painful strain filled his legs as he ripped his feet from the muck, working arduously to get away from the creature. Chased by the guttural growl, the cruel paws tearing up the earth, racing towards him, and helpless to defend himself, he screeched out for his mother.

Silence permeated the air.

Percy glanced over his shoulder and watched in terror as the creature leapt through the air at him. Too late: the razor-sharp claws sank deep into Percy's backside, driving him into the ground with prodigious force, driving the air from his lungs.

The fetid stink of the creature filled Percy's lungs; the foul odour was familiar, reminding him of an incinerator, and memories of the funeral home and his mother's cremation flooded back to him. The vile beast flung its head back and howled at the moon. Percy freed his right arm and reached out for the creature's neck. His fingers sank into the damp flesh, where clumps of matted fur and dead skin lopped from around its neck, spilling over Percy. A strangled scream escaped Percy's throat as lumps of the beast's hide peeled back in a gory transformation. A human form materialized from within the beast. Sticky black fluids drained from the exposed flesh, spraying everywhere, forcing Percy to squeeze his eyes shut.

When he opened his eyes, Mary Lee stood over him, naked except for the viscous fluids that coated her pale flesh and a sinister snarl that exposed the beast's teeth. Her mouth drew open, unhinging and swinging wide enough to engulf Percy.

"Help, Mom," Percy pleaded, praying to hear her voice respond.

Then everything went black.

Percy bolted upright, rigid and screaming savagely. Out of breath, he gasped as if breaking the surface of Deadman's Lake after seeing who could hold their breath the longest; his lungs ached the same.

The pregnant moon dominated the night sky. A blood red film coated its surface, casting an eerie glow over the forest. A bone-deep chill settled over Percy, his breath hanging in front of his face. It took him a moment to get his breath under control, his chest grateful for the reprieve.

A hand grazed his shoulders, rubbing in a circular motion. Sharpened, filed nails caressed his jugular.

"Did you have a nightmare, kiddo?" Mary Lee asked with a cackling burst of laughter, her sour breath hot against his neck.

IX. Inside

Covered in deep shadows and a soiled blanket, Percy gawked at Mary Lee. Unable to shake the ominous images from his nightmare, Percy shivered uncontrollably. He felt bugs crawling over him, even though he couldn't see much in the growing darkness. Putrid, damp air filled his nostrils and flooded his lungs. "Where-where am I?" Percy asked in a confused daze, coughing through the fluids built up in the back of his throat.

Mary Lee sat at the edge of the bed, and the springs groaned beneath her as she shifted her weight towards Percy. "You're home," she explained, her tone soothing.

Outside, the moonlight reflected off the mirrored surface of Deadman's Lake. Across the lake, he could see a roaring beach fire, the flames licking greedily at the faces crowded around it. Percy recognized the distinct racket of teenagers hooting and guffawing, accompanied by fits of drunken laughter. Realization struck him hard, clutching at his heart and holding his breath.

Percy kicked his feet, pushing the blanket off the foot of the bed. The stained white sheet slid off from the corner, revealing a soiled mattress. "This isn't my home," Percy answered. "This is your cottage, and I don't want to be here."

Mary Lee smiled at Percy, the radiant moonlight gleaming off her teeth. A twinkle of twilight caught in the mysterious depths of her pupil. "I don't mean your house. What I meant is that this is home. Family," she added.

"You're not my mother!" Percy shouted.

Desperate, he bolted out of bed and made a dash for the door. The rotten floorboards creaked beneath him, threatening to swallow him whole. Before he escaped, the door slammed shut in his face with a thunderous boom. Percy felt the delirious, rhythmic beating of the cottage's heart from his dream. The maddening melody threatened to drive him insane.

Percy stood inches away from the door, refusing to turn around. He reached out and seized the handle, spinning the doorknob, and yanked back. But the door refused to budge.

Mary Lee's gargled, cackling laughter rang out, drowning out the hideous harmony of the cottage's heart-beat. After her sinister laughter ceased, a heavy silence settled over the cottage. All that remained was the vibrating pulse of the cottage. When he turned around, he discovered she had vanished from the room. As he stared at the desolate space, a chill raced down Percy's spine. His hand fumbled for the door again, certain it would remain jammed shut. But when he pushed, the door swung open freely. A sudden, jolting racket of crumpling aluminium sent Percy's heart racing, the beats blending together into a droning buzz.

"Don't you want to stay with your mother?" Mary Lee whispered, her voice bleeding out through the walls.

"Join us. Angie loves it here."

With his eyes closed, Percy covered his ears and screamed, willing himself to wake up from this never-ending nightmare. When he removed his hands, he heard the breeze gusting through the cottage as the curtains billowed outwards in the wind. It took him a moment to catch his breath and gather his thoughts. "It's all just a terrible dream. None of this is real," he said with conviction, trying to convince himself without success: his heart was still racing with fear.

Moonlight from the window at the end of the hall flooded into the narrow corridor. The light illuminated the decrepit state of the cottage, which leaned crookedly with the wind. Damaged frames hung from the wall, with their pictures captured inside. Percy forced himself to pass the portraits, fighting to avoid the eerie eyes glaring back at him. At the end of the hallway at the top of the steps, a family portrait dangled from its hook.

"This can't be real," Percy muttered to himself.

Inside the golden frame, captured in vivid colour and surrealism, rested the Benoit family portrait from Percy's living room taken over five years ago. His mother's vibrant red dress was sullied by blood red streaks with her smile twisted into a ferocious grin. Ben stared at Percy with feverish intensity, his eyes two blazing embers that glowed red hot. Replaced by a more mature version of himself, a drugged-out Percy stared off vacantly into space; drool ran down his chin and soaked into the collar of his dress shirt.

From downstairs, Percy heard the faint sounds of a baseball game on television. A gregarious cheer rang out as the deafening crack of a bat thundered from the television; the sound was so clear Percy could have been sitting in the bleachers at the ball field.

"Is anybody down there?" Percy called out, making his way down the stairs.

The landing intruded on the main floor, taking up space in the middle of the living room. Bright light streamed from the television, revealing the filth covered floors. In the corner, dejected Blue Jay's players occupied the television screen as the Yankees celebrated behind home plate. Sitting back on to Percy, a man wearing a Yankee's ball cap watched the game. Stray strands of fabric torn from the tattered chair hung loosely over the floor, doing little to conceal the discarded beer cans littered all around it, as deep scratches covered the curved wooden legs and arms of the chair. Percy made his way around the chair, the figure sitting in the chair remaining hidden from view until he rounded the corner.

"Ben?"

Slumped in the armchair, Ben stared vacantly at the television. Globs of blackened, dried blood stained his face and undershirt. The skin had turned a greyish green and slid down his forearms and drooped, forming folds at his wrists. Red blotches stained his skin. Tiny maroon rivers spread out from the blemishes in a spiderweb pattern, crossing across his skin and feeding other scars. A viscous red slash opened his throat from ear to ear; his exposed Adam's apple crawled up and down his throat as he drew in haggard breaths.

"You're finally home," Ben said, his throat dry and gravelly, the words garbled and fueled by anger. He stood up from the chair and staggered forward, his feet scraping across the frayed area rug. "Get over here now, boy," he demanded.

Overhead, the floorboards creaked and groaned as rapid footsteps raced down the hallway, taking an impossibly long time to reach him; the sounds rushed forward, then receded. Percy twisted into the corner, keeping one eye on Ben and the other on the top of the stairs. Strained breathing from Ben echoed off the cottage walls, slithering closer, forcing Percy to inch his way back up the stairs until he found himself halfway up; caught in a dangerous position.

"Stay away from me!" Percy demanded, pointing his finger at the ghoulish figure taking Ben's form. "And don't you take another step!"

A deep grumble emanated from Ben's stomach, a sinister sound rising through phlegm: laughter. But the figure halted, swaying on his unsteady legs. Not wanting to become trapped on the staircase, Percy headed back down. Ben stared at Percy, his eyes two large drops of swirling oil. Blackened sludge tracked down from the creature's bloodshot eyes and over its rotten cheek; a devilish tongue lashed out of its bloodied mouth, lapping up the viscous fluids. With a burning intensity, the fiendish figure watched Percy. But for some unknown reason, it obeyed, allowing Percy to step past and reach the door.

A calming coldness from outside blew in as Percy yanked the door open. Before he stepped outside, Percy paused in the doorway, sensing the demonic soul from upstairs nearby. He glanced over his shoulder, his eyes growing wide with a typhoon of emotions that crashed over him. A powerful burst of wind ripped the door from his hands and slammed it off the side of the cottage, sending a shudder throughout the entire foundation.

Ben found his way back to his chair, his gaze glued to the ball game. Beside the armchair, a woman stood, her palm resting on the rotting shoulder of the vile creature slouched in the chair. Long coils of crimson hair, streaked by strands of grey, contoured the woman's face. A pair of tired but vivid sapphire eyes peeked out from behind the curtain of hair as a gentle smile sent a wave of wrinkles across her lovely face; her lipstick was a familiar, vibrant red. Dressed in a floral sundress, the woman standing beside Ben didn't belong in this hellish nightmare.

"M-mom?" Percy stammered, backing away. One foot rested in the house and the other planted on the dilapidated porch.

"Percy, come give your mother a hug." His mother's ethereal voice filtered through the false figure's throat. But it still warmed his heart to experience her sweet voice in his ears once more.

No longer afraid, Percy stepped back inside. He knew that if he didn't confront his fears now, he would never know what happened to his mother. Fueled by adrenaline, he faced the skin walker, determined to get answers and put his personal demons to rest.

From the darkness outside, something snatched Percy and hauled him out of the cottage, sending him tumbling backwards down the steps before he could confront the skin walker.

X. Text Message

Percy landed hard on the packed earth, the impact sending a shudder through his left shoulder that rattled his spine, driving the wind from his lungs. His cheeks turned bright red, bordering on purple from a prolonged lapse of oxygen. The colour returned to his complexion as he managed to catch short sips of air. His ribcage ached, and his lungs burned; the rapid breaths did little to ease his condition. Confused, Percy gawked up at a starlit sky where the silvery light of the moon beamed down on him. He craned his neck up, gawking up at the rickety porch of the cottage; the door closed over.

"What the hell are you doing?"

Percy rolled his head to the side, staring up at Damien. "Angie is in there somewhere," Percy said, wheezing as he sprung to his feet, then grimacing as a wave of pain radiated from his shoulder.

Damien laughed uneasily, noticing Percy's precarious state of mind. "Are you sure you're alright?"

"Angie's inside that cabin; the skin walker has her," Percy said, the words raced over his tongue, fumbling over each other.

"Angie is home," Damien announced, holding up his

phone. The LED screen emitted a soft white radiance.

Percy leaned in close, reading over the conversation, not taking in the conversation but scrutinizing over the time. None of this made sense to him; he double checked his watch. "I just heard her," he said, his voice trailing off. "If I find out you're a part of this, I swear to God—"

"I just got that message from her five minutes ago," Damien said, his voice heavy with concern. "There's no way she could be in there."

"But..." Percy stammered, turning to face the cottage, his gaze drawn towards the window. A faint trace of moonlight illuminated the interior of the cabin. He could see moving boxes littered across the floor, heaped in organized piles, and cleaning supplies strewn about the room. Some boxes on top lay opened, the flaps hung open like giant jaws in darkness, as articles of clothing dangled out of the box with sleeves and pant legs that mimicked limbs hung out of the gaping mouth.

"Let's get out of here," Damien said, laying a hand in the crook of Percy's elbow, trying to guide him back towards the path.

"What are you doing here?" Percy refused to turn his back to the cottage door, expecting that vile creature to burst out at any moment.

"I went to the tree house. But when I discovered you weren't there, I searched the trail for you."

"Why would you come here?" Percy asked, his voice quivering. Something drew them here; but what?

"You're obsessed with Mary Lee. It's not healthy, dude. Stalker," Damien added under his breath.

Percy patted his pocket, searching for his phone. He

withdrew it, discovering the screen pitch black. "Dead," he growled. "Can you send Angie a text?"

"Really?" Damien said, then sighed. "Fine, if it will shut you up." He unlocked his phone; the soft white glow cast deep shadows beneath his eyes, making them appear sunken deep within his skull. "What do you want me to ask her?"

"Anything," Percy replied, continuing, "I just need to know that she's okay."

"Whatever, man. I think you're overreacting. But like I said, if it will put your mind at ease," he said, grinning.

Percy watched intently as Damien hit send. Not really knowing what to expect, Percy's eyes sauntered back to the cottage. A dying glimmer of blue light captured his attention. "Did you see that?"

"See what?" Damien asked, annoyed and intrigued all at once.

"A flash of light. From inside the cottage," Percy said, his finger thrust at the window above the porch. "Just as you sent the text message to Angie."

"Maybe Mary Lee is inside and checked her phone," Damien answered, his eyes rolling as he did.

"It can't be a coincidence," Percy stated. "There's no way that Angie's phone isn't in there."

"Come on, Percy, let's go back to the tree house," Damien said, his tone distracted.

"Send another text," Percy demanded. "I know that Angie's in there and she's in trouble." Both boys peered up at the second-floor window as Damien sent another text. An intense blue light reflected off the window as Angie's phone hummed.

"Hole-Lee-Fuck." Damien said, flabbergasted.

"Jesus Christ," Percy said, his voice wavering. "We have to go get her."

"Wait," Damien called out as Percy mounted the stairs, grabbing a fistful of t-shirt. "There's no way I'm going in there."

"She's in danger," Percy announced, struggling against Damien. He twisted his body low, jerking his torso backwards, slipping out of Damien's grasp. But his momentum carried him into the first step before his feet could adjust. He hit the stair with his shin; slivers of the board dug into the flesh of his leg and scraped the length of his shin bone. With a grimace, he pulled himself up using the banister; it threatened to collapse beneath the pressure of Percy's weight.

Damien took a single step towards Percy, then halted dead in his tracks; his jaw hung open, and his eyes grew wide. "Was that door always open?" Damien asked, knowing the answer but ignoring the truth.

"No," Percy said without a shadow of doubt to cloud his statement. He turned towards the open door, staring into the dim lit of the moon creeping in between the open curtains.

"It must not have been closed over," Damien lied to himself. "And the wind blew it open."

"Angie!" Percy called out, cupping his hands and funneling his voice into the cottage. Still standing at the base of the stairs, he leaned forward, his leg muscles tensed and ready to spring back if something sprung out at him from the darkness. He put up his hand, motioning for Damien to wait.

Damien obeyed without objection.

With every step, the ancient wood groaned and creaked, shifting beneath his meager weight. A stale stench of rot and mold wafted from the open door, pouring from the gaping hole in a cascading stream. Percy made his way inside, every sense on high alert. His eyes wandered through the kitchen, searching for a sign of Ben in the shadows. A carton of apple juice lay on the table; the straw smeared with bright crimson lipstick.

"Everything okay in there?" Damien called out from the safety of the driveway.

Percy wandered into the living room, ignoring his friend. The seat where Ben had sat, watching the baseball game, was empty now; flimsy boxes occupied the vacant corner of the landing leading upstairs. Not convinced they were empty, Percy took deliberate steps towards them, anxiously monitoring them for any sign of movement. Somehow, the room loomed large before him, stretching impossibly long within the confines of the small cottage.

A fire ignited in the hearth, casting the room in a glaring red glow. Upstairs, Angie screamed, her voice shrill and strained. Embers burst from the fireplace, scattering across the floor. The first signs of smoke filled the air, choking Percy. Led by instinct, he stomped his feet over the embers, trying to prevent the cottage from going up in flames. A series of crackling sparks spat smoldering orange flankers across the furniture.

The heavy smell of wet, burning fabric flooded Percy's nostrils. But he refused to turn tail and run away. Determined, Percy charged towards the stairs, calling out to Angie. He made it halfway up the stairs when he heard a thunderous splintering crack. Broken boards fell into the darkness, clattering the entire way down. Momentum carried Percy forward, and gravity grasped at his ankles, yanking him down. His chest slammed into the edge of the next step, and his hands slapped off the wooden surface for a moment before gravity won, hauling Percy down into the darkness below the stairs.

XI. Under the Stairs

Without warning, Percy landed feet first on the hard packed dirt; his knees drove into his chest. With the wind forced from his lungs in a silent shriek, his toneless cry for help was swallowed whole by the engulfing blackness. The stench of wet soil and rotten wood soured the air, creating the peculiar aroma of Deadman's Lake. His lungs were saturated by the dampness supplied by the nearby lake. Something slimy squirmed over his hands, crawling over his skin in a parade of tiny legs. Percy jumped to his feet, brushing himself off frantically, unable to rid himself of the creeping sensation; a tangle of spiderwebs caught in his hair.

A faint trickle of light reached the stone wall above him, taunting him. He jumped up with his arms outstretched: just out of reach. "Damien!" Percy bellowed, his voice echoing off the hollow wall.

No response.

Cursing, Percy reached out for the wall, allowing his fingers to trace the grimy stone as he inched deeper into the darkness and away from the light.

Entombed in the unknown, Percy's heart fluttered erratically, skipping beats and racing without reason. Every step ventured further into a dismal abyss. The wall crawled with hideous shadows, and a droning buzz of insects and rodents hung in the air, making Percy's skin itch. Something brittle crunched beneath his feet, throwing him off balance; instinct forced his hand out. His fingers plunged into a wet crevice, and a trickle of warm liquid flowed over Percy's wrist and down his forearm. He jerked backwards, his backside striking a solid beam. Dust fell from the ceiling, settling into his lungs; he hacked a wad of phlegm into his hand.

Stumbling over something lodged into the earth, Percy banged his head off a beam; he fell hard onto his backside. The unknown object burrowed into his thigh, sending a wave of radiating pain shooting to his stomach. After rolling over, his fingers traced the object; the dry, jagged surface sent a shiver throughout his body. His pain was all but forgotten. That was when Percy noticed the light spilling over the bare earth. In the foreground, the porch jutted out into the driveway. A section of lattice, damaged by the weather, lay half buried just ahead.

All sorts of horrid insects wriggled and writhed through the darkened soil; but Percy didn't care. He'd found his way out from underneath this damned cottage, and nothing would stop him now. Percy swallowed hard, his Adam's apple bobbing in his neck as he dry-swallowed his fear. The ability to see the bugs writhing and squirming didn't help; he clenched his eyes shut and shot his hand forward. When he placed his palm down, his stomach lurched as the hard shell of a beetle burst; a gush of innards spread over the delicate flesh of Percy's hand between the webbing of his thumb and forefinger.

Footsteps boomed overhead, a thunderous stampede fleeing the house. Methodically, Percy followed the vibrations. A sliver of moonlight fell on the dew-covered grass, offering hope of escape. He crawled forward on his hands and knees, the damp earth frigid against this bare skin.

"Hey there, Percy," a croaking voice rasped from thin air.

Frozen in place, Percy longed to enjoy the moonlight grace his skin just once more. Cocooned in the vast bowels of the cottage, a pair of sickly green eyes stared at Percy; he watched them watching him, studying him. The haggard, laboured breathing of the skin walker, near yet far, intensified into a shallow rhythm.

"Why don't you make yourself at home?" the skin walker cackled, the words sounding like they came from beneath the surface of Deadman's Lake.

A pair of red Nikes raced past the opening, snapping Percy's attention away from those hypnotizing green eyes. "Get away from me!" Percy barked at the aberration before turning his head back to the opening and yelling, "Wait for me!"

"Give it up, boy," the skin walker took on Ben's haggard, cruel tone. "The only person who ever loved you is dead. Come, join us."

"Never!" Percy howled, his hands and knees working in unison. He dragged himself towards the light.

Behind him, the high-pitched sound of nails scrapping over rock raced towards him. The jagged tips of a clawed hand bit into Percy's calf. He screamed out in pain, rolling over onto his backside. The skin walker's decrepit arm jutted out from the shadows. Exposed muscle and sinew dripped blood and yellow puss over the ground. The reptilian eyes remained in the abyss, glaring at Percy from the unknown.

"Let me go!" Percy demanded, kicking his boot into the creature's face; a dull thud echoed, and he felt the flesh give way to bone beneath his blow.

The skin walker let out a vicious, growling yell, but relinquished its grip on Percy. Not wasting his opportunity, Percy scrambled towards the opening. Without hesitation, Percy lunged through the hole, the broken boards scraping at his shoulders as he shoved himself through.

"Percy?" Damien called out, surprised.

Percy glanced over his shoulders, scanning for the emerald glow of the skin walker's eyes. When he convinced himself that the skin walker didn't pursue him beyond the walls of the cottage, Percy made his way to his feet.

"What the hell happened to you?" Damien asked as he reached out and grabbed Percy by the shoulders.

They locked eyes: Percy's set and determined, Damien's wide with fear of the unknown. Damien's nose scrunched, and his lips curled into a deep-set frown. He traced the contour of Percy's neck with his index finger, pressing hard against the flesh to scrape off a layer of grime. Disgusted, Damien held his finger between them. Flakes of grimy black gunk coated his pink flesh.

"Did you find her?" a voice called from the end of the driveway.

"No," Damien called out over his shoulder. "But I found Percy." He turned his attention back towards Percy. "What happened to you, man; you vanished for hours!"

"I fell into the basement—" Percy began, then paused.

"Wait, did you say hours, as in plural?"

"Did he say where my sister is?" an angry voice barked.

"Who's that?" Confused, Percy's vision blurred. Suddenly, he felt exhausted, and his eyes grew heavy.

"Angie's brother, Stan, called me this morning when his sister didn't come home."

"Where is she, you bastard?" Stan snapped, grabbing Percy by the collar. "Just tell me."

Percy leaned away from Stan's grip, his shirt ripping with a shredding rapport, but he stood his ground against the older boy. "She's in there." Percy thrust his hand towards the cottage, then turned his attention to Damien.

"There's nobody in there," Stan snarled, shoving Percy backward. "We went looking for you and all we found was her damn cell phone." He held it up high, making sure Percy got a good view. "Bet you wish you didn't leave that behind."

"What are you talking about?" Percy demanded.

"I think you did something to my sister," Stan growled, taking a step towards Percy.

Defiant, Percy squared his shoulders to Stan and said, "I did nothing to her."

Damien wedged himself between them; Stan drove them both back with ease. If he really wanted to, he could have shoved Damien out of the way. Percy did his best to remain on his feet, doing his best to avoid tripping over any hidden hazards.

"I realize you're mad," Percy said, doing his best to remain calm. "None of this makes any sense to you and you're lashing out. Trust me, I get that. But I'm not your enemy. You need to believe me."

A series of chimes interrupted the tense scene. All at once, their phones turned on, ringing at full volume, and the scenes turned into a blazing glare. They all tried to turn off their phones with no success. The phones emitted a high-pitched tone that forced them to cover their ears; Damien dropped to his knees, throwing his cell into the tall grass.

"Jesus Christ!" Stan screamed over the deafening blare. "Make it stop!" He dropped to his knees and covered his ears with his hands.

A blinding white light beamed from the cottage windows, seizing the boys within its grasp. Percy's cell phone blistered, becoming too hot to hold. He dropped it into the grass; the dew sizzled.

An eerie silence fell over Deadman's Lake, and the ethereal glow washed over them. Despite the white-hot intensity, an icy chill ravaged the boys, and Percy's teeth chattered.

The light lifted from the cottage, and tendrils of fog rolled out from the windows and door, seeping between the cracks, snaking towards the boys. A rumble from beneath the ground rattled Deadman's Lake, wrecking havoc on the glossy surface, sending a series of sloshing waves crashing against the beach. High in the night sky, the light formed a bright white ball that burned with feverish intensity, hiding the stars and moon from view. Waves and streaks of varied-coloured lights shot out from the centre of the fake sun. Slowly, they took shape.

Transfixed by the light show, the boys stood silently, their mouths gaped open in wonder and fear. As the lights pushed outward from the artificial sun, the wind whipped through the trees, rustling the branches in a clamorous racket. Then, as the beams of light returned to their origin, the wind sent white caps across the lake.

White, blue, and yellow beams of light swirled together, forming a torso and limbs. Jagged lines of red shot through the emerging head, and with a thunderous clap, the light exploded, and the colour turned to dust that drifted towards the boys in a misty haze. The wind caught the falling debris, ushering it out and over Deadman's Lake. It swirled in the air in a mesmerizing cyclone before falling into the lake.

The light vanished from the sky without warning as the stars and moon crept back into the night. Percy let out a breath of air he hadn't realized he'd been holding, sucking in a mouthful of air and drawing it deep into his lungs: the air tasted bitter, coppery. A thunderous belch from the lake sent a bubble of water cascading out from the centre, the ripples racing towards the shore in uneven waves.

There were forms taking shape beneath the surface.

"What the hell?" Damien muttered, his voice shaken.

Ghastly figures emerged from Deadman's Lake: a mob lumbering towards the cottage in a throng. Waterlogged, their pale grey skin drooped and sagged from their bones. Black blemishes riddled their bodies. Festering wounds dripped vile fluids over the shore, leaving a greasy trail behind them.

The boys huddled together, turning their attention towards the staggering ghouls. An army of skin walkers trudged over the craggy shore in a demonic parade. Their haggard breath whispered to them, telling them horrible things as they marched closer. The boys backed away in unison, an unspoken bond forming between them in their time of need: survival instincts taking charge.

A shrill scream tore the air, shattering the macabre symphony of shambling corpses.

"Angie?" Stan called out, breaking formation and turning towards the cottage. "Wait for me!"

Damien and Percy spun around as Stan sprinted towards his sister. He called out for her as she vanished into the woods, her hysterical screams leading them.

The three boys followed Angie into the forest, Percy gaining ground on Stan while Damien fell far behind. Percy's footfalls hammered the ground as he sprinted past Stan. The forest closed in on him fast. Disoriented in the darkness, Percy slowed his pace.

"Where... did she... go?" Stan asked out of breath, panting as he caught up to Percy.

"I lost her," Percy said, his eyes searching the ground for signs of Angie's path.

Damien stumbled upon the boys, gasping for air. "Those things just..." he started, before running out of breath. He leaned against a pine tree to catch his breath before continuing, "They vanished into the cottage."

"What the hell is going on?" Stan asked again.

Percy spotted a disturbed cluster of bushes. "I think she went that way."

"You're not thinking of following her?" Damien blurted out.

Stunned by Damien's selfishness, Percy glared at his friend. But remained silent, at a loss for words.

"Are you some cowboy now?" Damien asked Percy,

then turned to Stan. "You think you're going to find her by yourself? We need the police or the national guard!"

"I'm not abandoning Angie," Stan answered, his voice booming in the stillness of nature.

"Me neither," Percy stated.

"You guys are nuts," Damien said, shaking his head. "Now the cops will search for three people." Damien stomped out of the forest towards the dirt road.

Without another word spoken, Percy and Stan wandered deep into the forest after Angie.

XII. Angie

Percy led the way, his eyes scanning the forest floor as they trudged through the thickening foliage. Stan laboured to keep up, his breath heavy and erratic. A purple twilight provided a backdrop to the canopy of tree branches overhead. Sporadic, Angie's trail came and went, refusing to offer hope but demanding they follow. Dead branches snapped beneath their feet. A heavy dew formed on the tree branches, soaking into their clothes.

Nearby, an owl hooted a deep call that went unanswered. For no real reason, Percy followed the sound. The tree branches clustered together, forcing them to shove their way through. Percy inhaled the fragrant bouquet of the forest: the gentle hints of pine needles and moss was tainted by a rancid reek. He suppressed the urge to scream.

Frustrated and lost, Percy picked up his pace and stumbled forward until he spilled into a clearing. His feet tangled in a gnarled root and he slammed hard into a thorny bush. Sharp needles ripped at his skin, leaving superficial lacerations on his wrists and forearms. His right hand landed in something soft and warm; repulsed by the strange feeling, he yanked his hand back.

"Crap," Percy mumbled, rubbing his hand over his jeans.

"You alright?" Stan asked without an ounce of compassion in his voice. He glared at Percy as he pushed past without offering his hand.

Percy stared at his wrist. It was hard to tell in the darkness, but something wasn't right. He held up his hand, discovering a thick layer of gore coating his hand. a bitter, coppery taste filled his mouth. Bile raced up his esophagus, burning his throat and sitting in the back of his mouth.

"Stan," Percy called out, his voice weak. "Wait."

Annoyed, Stan turned back towards Percy, his arms folded across his chest. "What's the matter? Can't handle a little shit."

"It's not shit." Percy held up his hand as if it were an artifact on display in a museum.

Stan shook his head and rolled his eyes, muttering something incoherent under his breath. But he came forward to get a better look, and his eyes grew wide. Trembling, he reached out and his finger traced over Percy's hand. A red blotch stained the tip of his finger. As if the substance burned his fingers, he wiped it off on his shirt. Streaks of crimson stained through his soaked shirt.

"Where did you find this?" Stan demanded, his voice firm.

Percy stared at the bush. "I'll look."

Percy had to fight with his motor functions, forcing himself to crawl towards the bush. Stan loomed behind him, his footfalls heavy on the forest floor. Carefully, Percy pushed aside the thorny branches with one hand, then plunged his free hand into the bush. Concealed behind the veil of thicket, Percy felt a warm, squishy ball. When his fist closed around the unknown object, hot fluids oozed between his clenched fingers. With fearful caution, Percy dragged the clump out of the bush.

When Percy's hand emerged, he dropped the deep crimson sack on the ground with a wet plop. Tied off with butcher's twine, a loose bow rested atop the bag as it jiggled, the contents inside sloshing around. Percy covered his mouth with his hand; fighting the urge to vomit, he turned his head to the side and expelled the acidic liquid over a bed of decaying needles. When he turned his head back, Stan was untying the bow.

Percy cried out for Stan to stop. But it was too late.

The contents of the bag spilled out with a sloshing spurt. A mound of purplish black organs rolled out of the bag, leaving a vivid scarlet stain over the grass. Coils of white intestines unfurled and lashed out like a striking snake, forcing Stan to jump back. He collapsed to his hands and knees, heaving his guts out as he cried out.

Horrified by the grotesque scene, Percy turned his head towards the heavens and cursed God. Tears stung his eyes before they tracked down his cheeks. Behind him, Stan sobbed and called out for his sister.

A tree branch snapped and a silence fell over the clearing. Percy's head shot over towards the sound. His eyes scanned the edge of the trees for any sign of movement. Every hint of movement caused his breath to catch in his throat; he gulped it down and choked on it, gasping for air. Something caught his eye at the edge of the clearing; a shadowy form in the trees, swaying back and forth like a pendulum.

Stan howled a guttural cry at the moon like a wounded animal. Another branch snapped, closer this time. Then another, this time from behind them. A wind blew through the trees, and the branches clattered together as if battling each other. Hysterical, Stan stared up at the moon, both hands buried in his hair. His anguished cries were raw and fueled by rage.

"Get him out of here, Percy. Before it's too late."

Percy realized he should try to comfort Stan before he hurt himself. But he couldn't take his eyes off eyes of the shadowed form. Ignoring the warning, Percy left Stan behind and marched towards the shape.

"No!" his mother shrieks. *"Please!"*

As he neared the swinging shape, it took shape in the dim light. Angie's lifeless form swayed from a tree branch; it creaked methodically with the dead weight. Thick rope was wrapped around her neck and slung over the branch in a diabolical series of tangled knots. A gaping black mess stained her dress, while ropes of scarlet viscera dangled from the savage wound. With her stomach removed, Percy could see the brownish yellow of her spine. Her skin hung loosely from her frail frame. Deep crimson tracks ran up and down her limbs, drawing Percy's attention away from her terrified, hollow expression.

Black, criss-crossed thread poked out of the red, sore flesh. A shudder of realization gripped Percy as he realized someone had stitched her skin back together. A thick, black track ran from her sternum and vanished into her soiled dress. More tracks covered her body, branching off the main one like arterial turnoffs from the main highway.

Angie's lifeless eyes gravitated towards him, her

mouth open in an accusing scream. Her cheeks sagged from her skull, her eyes sunk deep in the socket, with folds of skin crumpled together at the base of her neck. Her jet black hair was a stark contrast to her pale complexion, and a shimmer of moonlight danced in her hair. Scarlet tracks stained her pale her cheeks.

An agonized screech turned Percy around. Wide eyed, Stan held his hands over his gut, his shirt turning a deep red underneath. Suddenly, he lifted into the air, and he tried to call out.

Blood gurgled past his lips and splattered over the ground. His eyes rolled into the back of his head, leaving the whites behind to stare back at Percy; the glow of the moon illuminated them, giving Stan an eerie aurora. Then he glided forward, his boots scraping off the forest floor as he inched closer.

A wet, tearing pop exploded Stan's chest outward in a vicious display of power and gore; he collapsed into a heap. Behind Stan's mangled corpse, Angie stood there, a crooked smile twisting her face.

"Hey, Percy," Angie cackled, a wicked smirk bared her filed teeth.

Her flesh was now a series of vicious scars and rivers of black thread holding patches of skin in place. Something slithered behind her flesh, sending ripples and bulges over her face. When the bugs cross over the stitches, the thread would snap and tear at the seams; patches of skin peeled back from the flesh beneath. Tendrils of blackened blood oozed from the sore wounds.

"*Run!*" Percy's mother screamed with a dreadful sense of urgency.

And Percy did.

XIII. The Light

Drawing in a deep, haggard breath, Percy bolted through the dense forest.

Tree branches slapped him in the face, scratching at his exposed flesh. His feet ached as each step sent an excruciating jolt up his spine. Footsteps reverberated behind him, pursuing him through the forest: Angie's footsteps.

"Come back, lover!" Angie called out, her voice hoarse and pained.

Unable to bear the sight of Angie's maimed cadaver, he kept his eyes forward, refusing to glance over his shoulder as she called out for him. His lungs burned and his muscles cramped, but he pushed himself forward, running blindly through the woods, knowing that if he faltered even for an instant, she would catch him.

"I thought you wanted me!" Angie chortled, her laughter shrill and unnerving.

Already out of breath, Percy couldn't spare a word in response. His ribcage was aflame with searing hot pain, his heart hammering off his breastbone. He didn't think he could keep running much longer.

"There's nowhere you can hide."

"Stop running away from me."

"Now I'm getting mad." Angie's voice resounded in the still night air.

The rancid stench of diseased flesh poured from Angie's mouth with every word she spoke, her fetid breath forcing bile to race up his throat, burning the lining in his larynx. Percy felt her closing the gap between them, her footsteps slapping the ground with ruthless intensity.

In the distance, Percy could see a fluttering light at the edge of the lake. It appeared desperately far away; but something drew him towards the flickering flame. Now, changing directions in a sharp turn, he headed towards the burning fire in a straight line. Not fooled, Angie pursued, her haggard breath hot on his neck as she neared.

A sharp pain stung Percy as Angie raked her nails down his backside, her jagged nails shredding bright rivers of red into his flesh. She made another swipe, this time tearing a strip of flesh off Percy's elbow as she cackled maniacally. He could hear her sucking on her fingers and smacking her tongue off her lips as she slipped her bloodied fingers in and out of her mouth.

"I want to taste more of you," Angie giggled.

Desperate to shake her off his tail, Percy darted to the left and then dashed towards the right. Somehow, he gave himself enough distance to escape her next blow; her fist hacked through the air with a swift *swoosh*.

With a renewed sense of hope, Percy's legs pumped faster, his feet lighter as he made one final frantic dash for the flame. As he got closer, he could see someone holding the torch, their body a nefarious silhouette engulfed in the shadows. Doubt flooded his mind as the shadowed form turned towards him and rushed towards him.

"Percy!" A familiar voice cried out his name.

"Help!" Percy pleaded. It took him a moment to register his friend's voice. "Please, Damien!"

The yellowish-orange flame cast a warming glow over Damien's face. They sprinted towards each other, the distance between them shrinking. Damien slowed down as Percy reached him, thrusting the torch towards Angie. She slithered away from the flame, hissing at it as she mingled into the blackness of the enveloping woodland.

"That flame won't keep you safe forever," Angie snarled from the shadows. "And when it dies, so do you."

"Get out of here, you witch!" Damien barked.

Out of breath, Percy panted and gasped for air, his chest heaving with exertion. Unable to speak, he yanked on Damien's shirt tail, trying to direct him back towards the lake. The torchlight flickered all around them, the flame fluttering as the breeze threatened to blow it out.

With his voice cracking, Damien shouted, "Stay back or I swear I'll burn down every tree in Crooked Creek."

Vehement amusement greeted his hollow threat. Even Percy didn't believe his friend. Harbored within the darkness, Angie lurked out of sight, tree branches snapping all around, above and below. Her decrepit shadow jerked, keeping to the edge of the light, tracking them as they backed towards the lake.

"Don't tempt me," Damien snarled, holding out the torch towards a spruce tree.

"You don't have the guts!" Angie shouted at Damien from high above.

Percy put his hand on Damien's backside. He could

feel his entire body trembling with fear. "Give me the torch," he whispered in Damien's ear.

"What are you two lovebirds gossiping about?" Angie guffawed.

Without hesitation, Damien passed Percy the torch. The heat poured from the blazing bundle of rags, scorching the top of his hand; he understood why Damien gave up their only form of defense without putting up a fight.

"Last chance," Percy said, adding a harsh edge to his threat. He held out the torch, the orange glow inches away from the spruce tree.

Damien stood behind Percy, his hand stabilizing Percy's elbow.

"Do it," Angie taunted Percy, adding, "you fucking chicken."

The flame kissed the needles: a faint, stale stench of smoke filled the forest as the needles popped and sizzle as the fire ignited, fanning from branch to branch until the fire crackled and roared. Angie screeched in contempt, her shrill cry fading away.

"Dude." Damien spun Percy around so that they faced each other. "We gotta put that out before the entire forest burns down."

"Fuck that," Percy said without remorse. "There's no way I'm letting it die out until dawn. Besides, there's no other trees close enough to catch fire. So there's no real danger here. I'm just going to enjoy the warmth and bright light."

Percy passed Damien the torch, then edged closer to the fire and held out his hands, warming them in the blazing heat. A pillar of smoke raised into the sky as the flames devoured the branches. Steam hissed and bubbled from the trunk of the tree, and a loud cracking pop sent a shower of flankers into the air; a knot in the tree shot into the air and fizzled out as it landed on the damp grass. In the soft glow of the flames, Percy felt secure, basking in the warm embrace. An intimate physical state that made him reminiscent of his mother.

"So, what do we do now?" Damien stood beside Percy, holding the flame out towards the forest to hold the darkness at bay.

"We wait and pray that the fire burns until the sun comes up."

"But we've seen Mary Lee in the daytime. They're not vampires who can't tolerate the sunlight," Damien argued.

Percy stared into the dancing flames, unblinking. He sighed and shook his head. "Don't you think I know that? Whatever they are, they're more powerful at night. And I don't think they can hurt us during the daytime."

"Are you sure?"

"No," Percy answered, with no real confidence in his tone.

"I don't think I can make it through the night without sleep. I'm exhausted." Damien sulked.

Nearly choking on a fit of laughter, Percy swallowed down an enormous lump in this throat. "Tell me about it." Percy decided against mocking Damien or comparing who had a worse night. "Maybe we should sleep in shifts."

"My thoughts exactly," Damien said, searching the surrounding ground. He kicked at the grass, searching for roots. When he found a clear patch, he laid down; it reminded Percy of a cat kneading. "Sorry, but I won't last. I need to sleep first."

Percy checked the time, calculated how long until sunrise, and divided the night into two shifts. "I'll wake you in three hours."

Dawn refused to rise; a perpetual twilight loomed overhead. Percy gawked down at his phone, his eyebrows scrunched up at the time displayed on the screen. Time crawled past, unbearably slow, maddening. Only twenty minutes had passed since Damien fell asleep, snoring and whimpering in a troubled sleep, his legs twitching. He kept rolling over. Fighting sleep, Percy's eyelids grew heavy, and his head dipped down so that his chin rested on his chest; he pinched himself on the back of the hand so hard he drew blood.

From somewhere deep in the forest, he could hear voices whispering back and forth; Percy could only pick out bits and pieces of the conversation. But he heard enough to know that once the light died, they'd be in trouble.

"They can't run forever."

"Percy can't hide from us."

"I'm going to eat his liver."

"You can have whatever you want as long as you leave me those sweet cheeks. I'm going to eat them up."

Percy checked his phone again, noticing that his battery life had drained far more than it should have in half-an-hour; he didn't think that the battery would last to set off his alarm. Damien rolled over and groaned a long, pitiful sound. Percy stared at his friend, hoping that he would wake. Still asleep, Damien's lips moved in a jumble of incoherent consonants and clustered of vowels.

"*Keep the fires burning no matter the cost,*" his mother's voice spoke to him.

Alert, Percy jumped to his feet and twisted around. "Please help us, Mom," he begged. He staggered towards the sound of her voice. Just beyond the orb of light cast by the fire, the silhouette of his mother waited for him.

"*There is plenty of dry wood just over here. That's a good boy, come to mother.*" With her arms outstretched, she used her hands to usher Percy into her embrace. Delicate hints of his mother's lavender perfume mixed with the fresh aroma of the pine needles and dew. "*I've missed you, Percy.*"

"I missed you so much, Mom." Percy sprinted forward; his shoes never seemed to touch the ground beneath him.

"*Stop!*" his mother's voice screeched at Percy from inside his head.

A root wrapped around his foot, yanking Percy to the ground; he bit his tongue, his mouth flooded with the coppery taste of blood. He glanced up, searching for his mother. But the decrepit, rotten corpse of Ben stood just at the edge of darkness, waiting for Percy with one hand behind his back.

"*I almost had the fucker.*" Ben snickered. Sullied ooze seeped from his tear ducts in misshapen globules. Bugs squirmed beneath his skin; his flesh tore away from the bone and slapped back into place with a wet plop as the creatures criss-crossed. His facial features distorted, the skin drooping from his skull in wrinkled flaps.

"*Stay away from my son,*" his mother's voice called out

from behind Percy, emanating from the smoldering fire. *"You can't have him."*

A discordant eruption of laughter simmered beneath a layer of phlegm in Ben's throat. *"But we already have him. It's time you realized you can't save him!"* Ben barked as the wind hissed, tearing through the forest. Branches ruffled together in a clattering thunder. The wind threatened to blow out the fire, the flames fluttering until only the red glow of cinders remained. Shrinking, the circle of light closed in on Percy and Damien.

"Mom," Percy said, his voice trembling as he shuffled back towards the dying light of the fire. "Help us."

"Little bitch, crying for his mommy. Wahhhh, Wahhh," Ben guffawed.

"I can't help you. You need to protect the flames at all costs."

"Damien!" Percy hollered. "Wake up!"

With a perplexed expression on his face, Damien sat up and rubbed the sleep from his eyes. "It's s-so dark," he stammered, sleep heavy on his voice.

"Find something to burn — anything." Percy barked orders.

As the light diminished, Ben stomped forward in an uncoordinated cluster of jerky movements, his entire body jutting and contorting, his joints creaking and cracking with every step. *"Just give it up, Percy; you're never going to escape. Join us,"* Ben said, shoving his face into the light; his flesh seared and blistered as the light touched it, melting away his rotten features. The flesh slid off his face, revealing the glistening white bone of his skull; cockroaches crawled out of his nostrils and tumbled onto the grass.

Percy screamed, "Damien, I need your help!" Everything he picked up from the ground was wet; when Percy put them next to the coals, they fizzled and hissed, sending acidic clouds of smoke into the air. Percy bent down low, blowing at the smoldering ambers; they glowed red, the kindling trying to ignite in a sizzling hiss.

"Got you now."

Damien dropped to his hands and knees beside Percy to help spark the flames.

"I won't make your friend suffer if you give up now."

A yellow flame sparked, wrapping around the kindling in a soft glow.

"I'm going to make you regret that."

The flames spread out, burning bright orange now, the fire igniting the tree trunk with a gregarious *whumpf*.

"Stop resisting us, Percy." Angie's voice joined in with Ben's.

"You can't win. Give up now," Mary Lee added.

"Fight it, son." Percy's mother's voice faded, drowned out by the pained symphony playing in the darkness.

With the flames roaring, the circle of light fanned outwards, pushing back the vile demons. Their screams surrounded them, coming at them from all angles. Defeated, the skin-walkers fell silent and fell back into the dismal abyss that hung over the forest, waiting for their next opportunity.

"Thanks," Percy said, panting.

Damien rolled over onto his back, staring up at the pitch-black night sky with unblinking eyes. "What time is it?"

"You don't want to know," Percy answered, glancing at his phone with a grimace.

Both boys remained vigilant, neither able to gather the courage to fall asleep. They used their bodies to block the wind from the smoldering embers as the tree burned down into ashes. Continually shifting, the breeze kept the boys occupied. Percy inclined his head back, staring up into the starless horizon, the pitch black expanse oppressive. With a worried tone he asked, "Is it just me, or is the sky falling down on us?"

Confused, Damien responded with another question. "What do you mean?"

"I don't know." Percy glanced at his phone and shook his head. "Check your phone for me. What time do you have?"

Damien's hands patted his pants pockets. A troubled expression scrunched up his facial features, his eyebrows touching and a cluster of wrinkles creasing his forehead. "I don't know where it is?"

"Damn it," Percy grumbled.

"What's wrong, Percy? Is there something you're not telling me?" Damien asked, his voice rattled with fear.

"It's only one-thirty."

"That can't..." Damien stammered. "How can that be possible?"

"I know. It should be dawn by now. We've been here for hours, but time has crawled by. And my battery is going to die at any minute."

A fallen tree branch snapped nearby, the sound of a gunshot in the hushed silence of the forest. Both boys twisted towards the sharp noise. Percy backpedaled towards the dying fire, the warmth weakening against his backside. A terrifying screech tore the silence from the forest; gale force wind rushed through the trees, rattling the tree branches overhead. Chaos reigned around them, washing over them in a torrent of horrific screams that carried on the wind.

Bitter cold winds swirled around them, leaves and debris dancing in tumultuous turmoil. A branch whistled towards Percy's head; he jumped out of the way just in time. It crossed the cyclone, catching in the current on the other side and continued its trajectory around the fading fire.

"What do we do?" Damien cried out, his arms raised to defend his face, peering out through the crack in his forearms.

Percy ducked as the cyclone hurled a rock at his head; it smashed against the burning stump, sending a volley of flankers into the air. The cyclone sucked the red fiery sparks into the blistering winds, the spinning air turning them white hot. Percy rolled over onto his side, watching helplessly as the circle of light collapsed inwards. Fits of laughter echoed just beyond the boisterous roar of the cyclone.

A smoldering ember struck the ground beside Percy; the chunk of wood fizzled out in the damp grass. Percy rolled over on his side, where a sharp object dug into his backside. His eyes searched the ground behind him, his fingers prodding through the wet grass; his middle finger struck the torch. With a clenched fist, he grasped it by the handle and held it up triumphantly.

Without asking for help, Damien joined Percy by the burning stump, doing his best to shield the torch. The cyclone stopped: debris fell to the ground with a resounding patter that reminded Percy of torrential rainfall. Quick bursts of wind attacked the stump at all angles, forcing the boys to scurry around the tree to protect the fading embers. Blasts of icy wind stabbed at their backs, attacking them with a savage intensity.

Percy welcomed the acidic stench of smoke as the soiled rag sparked, catching fire with a weak yellow flame. With urgency, Percy shielded the torch and said, "Help me."

Damien joined Percy, protecting the opposite direction with his body, wrapping his arms around Percy's waist in an awkward embrace. The wind stabbed at the torch, forcing its way through the cracks between the boys' bodies — but the flame refused to die out. An intense wave of heat poured from the burning rags as the flame strengthened into a brilliant orange globe. Defeated, the wind diminished until it became a harmless breeze.

"Let's get out of here," Damien said, tugging on Percy's sleeve.

Percy resisted Damien's guidance. "We don't need to run," Percy answered, his voice steady.

"But those monsters in the forest will get us," Damien begged, reaching out for Percy's wrist. Percy shifted his body, avoiding Damien's grasp while holding his ground. "What's wrong with you? I can't stay here and wait to die."

"I'm not asking you to do that." Percy stared through the flames at Damien, watching as deep shadows settled over his friend's face; Damien's eyes sank deep into their sockets, the bridge of his nose a sharp ravine. Every wrinkle on his face defined with decrepit detail, the dull glow made his skin turn ashen grey. A shiver raced down Percy's spine at the sickening sight of his friend.

"Then let's go."

"Alright, I'll go." Percy paused. "But we can't outrun them. There's no point in trying and I won't waste my energy — it's what they want."

"Fine, whatever."

Percy held the torch high, the orb of light stretching further into the forest. He turned back towards the forest and shouted a wordless cry.

"Follow me," Percy said with a grin afterwards. "You're going to want to see this."

"*Where are you going, lover boy?*" Angie cackled.

Percy walked towards Deadman's Lake. "You'll see," he called out over his shoulder.

"*So brave,*" Mary Lee chortled and swooned, "*my hero.*"

"*That's my son,*" Ben added, his voice filled with false pride.

Percy turned towards Damien and whispered into his ear, "Let's end this nightmare."

XIV. The Car

The pebbles shifted beneath their feet, clattering amongst each other as they tumbled towards the water. After following the beach for twenty minutes, the forest behind them grew reticent. Even though he wouldn't admit it, Percy felt better without their diseased cries calling out to him. When they rounded the corner, the beach made a giant horseshoe shape around the harbour. The short-cut to the cottage lay just ahead, but Percy knew he wanted to take the long way there; there were too many hiding spots along the forest trail for the creatures to lay in ambush.

The quivering reflection of flames drowned as they reached the lake's placid surface, the water devouring the light and refusing to give it back. A rancid, sour odour wafted from the lake, hanging in the still air; Percy tasted rotten meat in the back of his throat. Damien kept closer to the land, his nose scrunched up at the awful stench.

Damien stopped suddenly, the rocks making a clamorous racket. "Wait," he said, sounding out of breath. "Where are you bringing us?"

"I told you," Percy responded without waiting for Damien. "This ends tonight. I'm exhausted and terrified. I can't take this anymore. Either I stop them from torment-ing me or I die in that cottage. I can't do this anymore."

Damien rushed forward to catch up, not wanting to be left behind in the darkness. "But I can't do this. There's no way I'm going into that cottage, Percy. After the feeling I got the last time, I just can't do it." He caught up to Percy and grabbed him by the shoulder, spinning him around. His eyes were wet, tears welling in the corner of his eyes.

"I'm sorry, Damien," Percy said, his tone defiant. "There's no other option for me. If I back down now, they'll win. This is my only chance."

"I can't go with you," Damien answered.

"I'm not asking you to," Percy said, yanking himself free of his friend's grasp.

"You can't leave me out here without that torch," Damien pleaded, his voice shuddering with fear. "They're going to kill me."

Percy strode away as he spoke: "They don't want you. It's me they're after. If you don't want to help me, then just go back to your house and cushy lifestyle."

"That's not fair," Damien said, standing at the edge of the arc of light. "It's not my fault that your mother isn't here…"

Percy interrupted, cutting his friend off in mid-sen-tence. "You think my mother could have stopped these monsters?"

"These demons are inside your head because you re-fuse to accept the truth that has been right in front of you this whole time. You're too afraid to face it, so you've been running from it since the night your mother died."

Percy stomped forward and thrust his finger into

Damien's chest. "Then what are you so afraid of, huh? If this is all in my head, turn around and walk away. You know what; this is typical Damien. When things get tough and you can't joke your way out of it — poof! You're gone."

"Well, you know what? You've always been a head-strong asshole, Percy!" Damien yelled, swatting away Percy's out-thrust finger. "Even if I told you the truth, you'd never believe me."

"Do you have anything to say that's going to help me defeat my demons? Or are you just trying to guilt me into bringing you home where the monsters can't hurt you? Is that it?"

Damien paused, staring down at his feet and refusing to match Percy's gaze. "Not exactly. I can help you face your demons. But I can't help you beat them. Only show you the way."

"What are you rambling about, Damien?" Percy snapped. "I'm losing my mind here, and I need you to help me. All you're doing is having me go in circles. Are you offering to help me or not?"

Damien drew in a deep breath and let out a melodramatic sigh. "Follow me."

"I told you, I'm finishing this now!" Percy raised his voice with rage curdling his words. "There's no going back now."

"Just let me show you," Damien said, his voice eerily calm. "It will help you deal with your demons."

"Fine," Percy snarled, then added, "lead the way."

Damien turned around and started back down the beach, keeping just to the edge of the light. Angry, Percy followed close behind, cursing under his breath. From the edge of the forest, Percy heard footsteps following them. He tried to cast the light on them to scare them away; but the flickering glow died in the trees, the blackness not allowing the light to penetrate any further. Snickering laughter echoed nearby, enraging Percy.

"Come out and face me, you bastards!" Percy hollered towards the forest.

Damien kept going, the light following him as he went; the arc of light shifting to an elongated oval. An unseen force tugged at the torch, urging Percy to follow. "What's going on, Damien?"

"You'll see," he answered, his voice sombre. "It's just up this way." He pointed up an old trail that followed the river.

"Are you taking me to the old fishing bridge?"

"That's the way we are heading." Damien trekked through the underbrush that had invaded the trail.

"Don't go, Percy," his mother's voice rose inside his head. *"You don't have to see this."*

"See what?" Percy asked, speaking out loud.

Damien turned around with an incredulous expression on his face. "Did you say something, Percy?"

"He's just wasting our time. You know what you have to do to end this."

"I'm going back to the cottage," Percy grunted, forcing the words out of his mouth.

"It's not your mother, Percy," Damien said matter-of-factly. "Don't listen to it."

"And why the hell should I listen to you?" Percy snapped; his cheeks flushed red with anger.

Damien turned towards Percy with a blank expression on his face. "Because I'm going to show you something. Not what you want to see, but what you need to see. Before you face your demons, there's something you should realize. And you will not believe it until you see. Now, stop wasting your own time and follow me."

Stunned, Percy stood silent, the only sound coming from the wavering flames of the torch. Vanishing into the darkness, the hollow echoes of Damien's footsteps faded away. Percy cupped his hands and called out to his friend to wait up. When he didn't get an answer, he ran down the overgrown trail. Tree branches tore at his clothing, threatening to rip the clothing from his body. He fumbled through the familiar trail, his feet traipsing over known roots and hidden stumps without a second thought.

When he stepped out of the bush and into the clearing, Damien stood motionless beneath the bridge; a shadowed object lay strewn about his feet. Percy stumbled forward, his feet tangling in the deep underbrush. As he approached, the shape of a car formed before his eyes in vivid detail. "Damien, what is that?"

"Come closer. It will come into focus and will reveal itself to you."

The moonlight struggled to illuminate the car, concealing itself until Percy got right next to it. A bright red Honda Accord's bumper dug into the soft bed of the river, the back tires still spinning. Smashed beyond recognition, the front bumper lay beneath the rippling waves. The roof of the car pointed towards Percy, the grill a crumpled heap of metal facing him.

"Damien," Percy said, his stomach twisting into knots.

"Is this my mother's car? It can't be? Because somebody would have found it before now."

Damien remained silent.

"Mom!" Percy shouted out, stumbling forward; the water sloshed over his boots and rose to his knees as he waded into the deeper water. The bride jutted across the road, hanging precariously from the bank overhead. "Damien, what the fuck is this?"

"I can't tell you." Damien sighed, stepping aside. "You need to understand this for yourself."

"What if I can't handle this?"

"Then you'll never be able to face your demons," Damien answered.

"Damien!" Percy called out. "Where are you?"

He searched the riverbank, but Damien had vanished.

He trudged through the water, the ice-cold current stinging his legs and sending a shiver coursing throughout his body. With a cautious approach, Percy made his way towards the overturned vehicle. It didn't take him long to recognize the air freshener dangling from the rear-view mirror, or the Sponge Bob seat cover in the backseat.

"Mom?" Percy waded through the gushing current, the soles of his shoes slipping on algae growing over the rocks that lay on the riverbed. "Mom!" he screamed at the top of his lungs. He stumbled towards the front windshield, finding the cab vacant.

"Percy," Damien said, his voice isolated inside Percy's head despite the wide-open space.

"Why are you showing me this?" Percy demanded.

"Take this image in, absorb it deep into your hippocampus, and allow your memories to come to the surface."

"What the fuck?" Percy spat. He leaned in close to the windshield, exploring the cab of the car for any detail. "There's no one in this car. This can't be my mother's."

"Why not?"

"B-because," Percy stammered. "After six months, somebody would have found this car here. It's below the bridge. This can't be her. There's no way." Percy beat his fist against his thigh in frustration.

"Are you sure it's been six months?" Damien questioned.

"What are you talking about?"

"How can you be so sure, Percy?" Damien asked, remaining back on to Percy. "Think really hard about it. Hasn't this all seemed like a dream to you?" Damien paused, waiting for Percy to respond.

"I don't want to relive any of this; why can't you understand that it's been the most hideous experience of my life?"

"I appreciate that — but you need to witness this with your own eyes," Damien spoke softly. "Until you do, you'll never be able to face those creatures waiting for you."

With a wavering hand, Percy reached out and touch the shattered windshield. A jolting tremor coursed through his body, his vision a field of bright light. His entire body jerked as another jolt ravaged his body. The torch flew from his hand, twirling through the air before landing on the river with a hissing fizzle. Darkness flooded over Percy. When his vision cleared, he found himself on his back, staring up at a stranger leaning over him. Behind the stranger's contorted expression, a dull yellow moon hung in the sky; a cloud draped over the yellow orb and stars littered the night sky, casting a soft glow over the forest. Percy opened his mouth in a silent scream, incapable of producing a sound. The man rubbed two paddles together, and a buzz of electricity hummed in the air.

"Clear!" the man shouted with a concerned expression plastered on his face, pressing the paddles down onto Percy's chest.

His body twitched and a blanket of white feverish light filled his vision. As the veil lifted from his eyes, he leaned against the hood of the car, staring into the interior of the Honda Accord; a spattering of blood coated the steering wheel and dashboard. The reflection in the side-view mirror revealed the stranger from his vision, leaning over a body at the side of the riverbank. In the mirror, Percy noticed the man wearing a paramedic's uniform and holding a defibrillator. Percy spun his head around, his eyes falling on the empty bank.

"Damien," Percy whispered. "What's happening to me?"

"Focus now. Let the memory come back to you."

Slowly, Percy raised his hands to his face, his fingers digging through his knotted hair; he clenched his eyes shut and howled, willing the maddening images from his mind.

"You need to stop fighting against it, Percy."

Percy ripped a clump of hair from his scalp in frustration. Disheartened and terrified, Percy lost his balance and collapsed to his knees. He tilted his head back and opened his mouth wide , screaming into the tarnished chasm above. The babbling racket of the water rushing over rocks and around the Accord droned into his skull. Percy slammed his fists into the riverbed and leaned back on his heels. Vile and blood raced up Percy's throat and spewed from his lips, sloshing in the water with a sickening plop.

"Open your eyes, Percy, and tell me what you see," Damien said, as if nothing happened.

Willed by a force deep within, Percy obeyed. Vivid details revealed themselves; crumpled aluminum beer cans lay strewn about the car, the strap of Percy's baseball bag hooked around the headrest, the bag resting on the roof.

"I knew it," Percy snarled. "Ben killed my mother." Enraged, Percy bolted to his feet and dashed towards the darkness of the trail. His boots splashing through the frigid water as he raced past Damien. His friend turned away from him, staring off into the night sky. "Come on, Damien, I need you help."

Damien never followed. Before he left the clearing, Percy glanced over his shoulder and found the riverbank empty. The bridge ran over the babbling water, its railing still intact; but the car and Damien were nowhere to be found. Once again, Percy found himself alone in the darkness.

XV. The Cottage

With reckless abandon, Percy darted down the spiraling path towards the beach, an unknown force guiding him over the submerged roots and stumps. A dreadful silence blanketed the woods, pressing against Percy and weighing on his mind. The air, chilled and foul, threatened to fill his lungs and choke him. Just beyond the veil of darkness that hung over the forest, a dim light resonated in the distance, swelling and shrinking with a methodical cadence. Behind the dirty kitchen window, a flame fluttered and swirled in a lamp on the far wall.

As he approached the cottage, he could hear Angie calling out his name, and Ben's tyrannical snickering. When he left the forest, a fetid stench wafted out from Deadman's Lake, escorted by the macabre scent of decomposing flesh. Mary Lee sat on the stairs with her fingers entwined in a tangle of her bright red hair; her lips were a seductive, glossy crimson. The door swung open, and Ben lumbered out with a decrepit shuffle, his boots scuffing across the weathered wood. Ben took a spot beside her, his fingers tangled in locks of her curly hair, his arm draped over her shoulder.

"Took you long enough," Ben said, his voice gurgled

and thick. "Did you and your boyfriend have a delightful time together?"

An energetic burst of laughter erupted from Mary Lee. With a skewed grin, Mary Lee turned her attention towards Percy, her emerald eyes wild and alive. "Leave the poor boy alone, Ben, he's all alone and still doesn't understand what he's up against." Mary Lee stood up, her skirt riding up her thigh; she didn't bother to adjust it.

"Fuck you!" Percy screamed, spittle flying from his lips.

Neither of them paid any heed to his outburst. Ben draped Mary Lee's hair around his finger; he yanked a giant clump from her scalp and chewed it absently, his eyes fixed on something in the pitch-black sky. A trickle of blood dribbled down Mary Lee's forehead, the scarlet drop tracked down the contour of her nose and puddled on her upper lip. With a slow, rolling lick of her tongue, a euphoric expression crossed Mary Lee's face at the taste of her own blood.

Angry, Percy's hands clenched into fists, and he stomped up the driveway and towards them, his entire body tense and upper body coiled, ready to lash out. "You're going to pay for what you did to my mother," Percy snarled, drawing his fist behind his body, ready to strike out with every ounce of strength in his being.

In a broad arc, Percy unleashed his hatred for Ben as a devastating right hook. His fist connected with the rotten flesh on Ben's cheek; he savored the way it gave beneath the blow. A clout of blood flew from Ben's pursed lips and spattered over Mary Lee's white blouse.

With a shrill cackle, Mary Lee licked her lips and let

out an enraptured groan. "Are you going to do me next?" As she got to her feet, her joints cracked and popped, her legs faltering beneath her.

Not wasting the opportunity, Percy swept his right foot across the steps, kicking Mary Lee's legs out from under her. The back of her head smashed off the staircase with a wet smack, a gout of blood spurting from her ears. A crack opened the back of her head open, moonlight illuminating the exposed skull beneath layers of thick blood and cerebral fluid. Percy lurched backward, staring at Mary Lee in disbelief; her smile spreading from ear to ear.

"What are you?" Percy demanded.

A branch snapped behind him. Percy whirled around, finding Angie racing across the wet grass towards him. Percy turned to run, colliding into Ben's bony chest, both of them collapsing to the ground in a tangled heap; Ben's putrid breath was hot on Percy's neck. Percy struggled against Ben's grasp, his gnarled fingers clawing at his backside, and his jagged fingernails clawing at his flesh through his shirt.

Percy found his feet, tossing Ben to the side just as Angie slammed into him and sent him stumbling to the right, but he stayed on his feet. Angie leapt at Percy, wrapping her arms and legs around him; feverish heat drained from her sweaty flesh. He jerked his upper body, trying to toss Angie off, but somehow, she stayed on him, her hands clasped together over his chest. When he grabbed her by the wrist, her flesh peeled back and fell over her hands.

Ben's fingers clawed through the damp soiling, grasping handfuls of sod and tossing them at them, laughing louder with every striking blow. A clump of earth shattered over Percy's head, releasing a torrent of slithering bugs from the rotting soil. Terrified screams escaped Percy as he felt the bugs writhing all over him. He swatted at his face, rubbing his fingers through his hair; they fell from his scalp and withered in the wet grass, thousands of white grubs covering the ground now. When he squashed them beneath his feet, they ruptured open with a loud, snapping *pop* as long streaks of watery blood gushed from the grubs in spurts.

Mary Lee sat on the stairs, her hand sprawled out behind her as she leaned back, enjoying the show. Percy caught flashes of her as he spun around, Angie's nails clawing at his face, tearing strips of flesh from his cheeks and forehead; Ben reached out with deformed fingers, endeavoring to trip Percy.

"Get off me!" Percy barked, jerking his body to the right. The momentum carried him down, driving Angie into the soft earth: a muffled gasp escaped her throat.

Angie's grasp relinquished, Percy rolled off of her and away from Ben. Gasping for air, Percy stayed on his hands and knees, refusing to take his eyes off of the depraved creatures plaguing him. Ben sat with his chin tucked to his chest. Fresh clouts of blood oozed from the savage gash on his neck.

"So rough," Mary Lee said, winking at Angie.

Angie sat up, brushing the bugs off her soiled dress and said, "You should watch the next time he dreams about me. Nasty doesn't begin to describe this boy's fantasies." She winked at Percy with a flirtatious smile.

Percy stumbled to his feet, pressing himself up with the rest of his strength. "This ends tonight," he panted, out of breath.

"But your story is just beginning, dear." A voice jumped out of the shadows.

Percy cocked his head over his shoulder, keeping one eye on the cottage and one eye trained on the edge of darkness. "Who said that?" Percy demanded.

"Now, is that any way to speak to your mother?"

Percy's mother emerged from the blackened woods, her white dress billowing behind her in the gentle breeze. She strode towards Percy with practiced grace, the moonlight captured in her eyes. Percy turned to face her, stumbling forward with his arms outstretched, longing for her embrace. He wrapped his arms around her, pressed his face into her shoulder, and sobbed into her dress, his tears soaking the fabric. She squeezed Percy, running her fingers through his hair, and cooing gently in his ear.

In a state of disbelief, Percy pulled himself back, her hands latched together behind his back. "Is it really you, Mom?"

"Of course, Percy," she answered, reaching out and tracing his cheek with her finger.

"How sweet," Ben mocked in a high-pitched tone. "Precious baby boy, Percy finds his mommy."

A chorus of laughter greeted his imitation.

"What's wrong, Percy?" his mother asked with tender concern on her tongue. "Stop staring at me like that."

"Why are you so cold?"

XVI. Truth

A tributary of blood snaked out from under his mother's hair, tracking down from her scalp. In the dull light, her hair was a tangled, matted mess, and her skull deformed, her forehead caved in above her right eye.

"Mom," Percy whispered,."What is happening?"

"Percy," she sighed, taking a step back. "I think you're ready for the truth now." Stepping past Percy, she made her way to the cottage; the others vanished inside before she reached the staircase.

"Don't go in there with those monsters!" Percy called out, his hands outstretched for her; his shoes sank deep into the soft earth, fixing him in place.

"They're not my demons, Percy," his mother said, standing in the threshold. "They're yours." The savage wound on her forehead vanished, leaving the moonlight to glimmer on her pale complexion. With the wave of her hand, she brushed the hair back from her face, smiling gently at Percy. She danced into the cottage and closed the door behind her.

Alone, the breeze carried a horrendous stench off the lake, and the coppery tang of blood sullied his mouth and coated his nostrils. He stared down at the earth where the ground writhed with worms and spiders. His clothes, sullied with a gore, emitted the putrid odour of rotting flesh mixed with body odour. Along the beach, decrepit shadows lurched towards him, closing in on him; the sound of water pouring from their mouth and ears sloshed over the craggy shore.

Confused, Percy called out to his mother; his voice dying in the stale air. A pale yellow glow sparked behind the window, spilling outside and casting the ground in dancing shadow. Percy could hear the soft voice of his mother singing through the walls, drawing him in. Before he knew it, Percy stood on the staircase, the worn structure swaying beneath him. Afraid to go back, Percy threw the door open and stepped inside the cottage for the last time.

When Percy stepped inside, the pleasant aroma of bread baking rose from the stove. Sitting at the table, Ben held a handful of cards in one hand while drinking a beer with the other one. He laid the beer down and threw a red chip into the centre of the table and announced, "Calling your bluff."

Mary Lee raised the cards to cover her mouth and giggled, laying down a full house: aces over kings. "Beat that."

Disgusted, Ben tossed his cards down on the table and shuffled them back into the deck. "Take it," he said, waving his hand towards Mary Lee.

In the kitchen, his mother hummed a familiar tune as she busied herself with the dishes in the sink. Suds and bubbles danced in the air as her hands worked beneath the water. Her hips swayed back and forth to the tune in her head, slow and steady. Angie came down over the steps and took a seat beside Ben. Mary Lee shuffled the cards, flicked one across the table to Ben, then held one out to Angie; when she nodded her head, Mary Lee dealt her into the game they were playing.

"Mom," Percy mumbled. "What's going on here?"

His mother bent down in front of the stove with the door open, pulling out a loaf of bread. She laid it on the stovetop and removed her oven mitts, placing them in the drawer beside the stove.

"Mom," Percy said, raising his voice. "Answer me."

"Take your seat," his mother said with a firm tone. "And I'll fix you a warm slice of bread with butter, your favourite."

"I don't want any damn bread!" Percy shouted. "What I need are some fucking answers."

"That's no way to speak to your mother," Ben said, pushing his chair back and standing tall.

His mother motioned for Ben to take a seat. "Sit down, Ben, before you burst an artery."

"Can't be any worse than what he's already done to me," Ben grumbled, taking his seat.

Mary Lee placed the deck of cards on the table, discarding a card face down beside the pile and flipping over three cards. "Texas Hold'em, grab some chips." She pointed towards the empty seat; five cards waited for Percy.

"I don't want to play this game," Percy groaned.

"I never wanted to play with you," Angie said, her voice subdued. "But I felt sorry for you because of what happened to your mother. I should have never gone to that tree house to meet up with you. I knew it was a terrible idea." Angie lowered her head and sighed. "My brother warned me about you. And I should have listened to what everyone at school said about you since your mother died."

"Leaving with Mary Lee was your mistake," Percy accused her. "I don't know what she did to you, but I've been trying to save you ever since you left."

"There's no saving me," Angie said, tears welling in her eye.

"I saved her from you," Mary Lee said. "From the awful things you did."

Angered, Percy slammed his fist off the table; the chips bounced into the air and fell back down with a clatter. "Saved her from the awful things I did?" Percy laughed. "You're one delusional bitch." Percy turned towards Angie, staring at her with incredulity. "I don't know what your problem is. I never forced you to come to that tree house. You wanted to, just as bad as me."

Angie shook her head in defiance.

His mother rested a hand on Percy's shoulder, guiding him towards his seat. "Percy," her voice cracked, on the verge of tears. "Please, you're not well. Let us help you see the truth."

Percy jerked his body, brushing away his mother's hand. "You want me to sit down at a table with that animal?" Percy thrust his finger at Ben. "The man who killed my mother and tortured me for years?"

"Ever since the day you were born, I've been afraid of this," his mother said.

"Afraid of what?"

"Of what you would become," his mother answered.

She leaned against the kitchen counter, staring at Percy with tear-filled eyes. "Without me around to watch over you, the family disease took control of you."

"What are you rambling about, Mom?" Percy spat. "None of this is making any sense."

"Take your seat, Percy. I'll do my best to explain it to you."

Percy backed away from the table, his boots scuffing over the grimy linoleum kitchen floor. "You're not my mother," Percy announced. "This isn't happening. It's all in my head." He beat his fist against his forehead. "Get out of my head! You're not real!" He clenched his eyes closed and screamed.

When he opened his eyes, his mother had taken a seat in the living room, watching the television. The poker chips and cards lay strewn about the table, the chairs now vacant and no sign of his demons anywhere. A fire crackled nearby, the flankers popping from the wood and sizzling through the chilly night air, dancing across the windows all around. Percy felt a wave of heat crash over him, burrowing into the pit of his stomach and making him woozy.

"Come," Percy's mom patted the seat beside her on the cushion. "I'll explain everything to you. But you have to come quickly because your time in this realm is running out."

Obediently, Percy stumbled across the living room, the wood beneath his feet scorching hot. The acidic scent of smoke filled the room. Terror filled Percy's limbs with ice cold blood, the sludge coursing through his veins. "Mom, we need to get out of here now!" he screamed, rushing over to his mother and trying to haul her to her feet.

Surprised by his mother's tremendous strength, she yanked him down onto the cushion beside her. "It's too late, Percy. You can't go back out there anymore. I can save you, but you have to understand something first."

"What are you talking about?"

"Listen to your mother and you'll be fine," his mother's tone soothing despite the surrounding chaos. "I wish I could make this decision for you. But you have to decide by yourself."

Disoriented by the smoke and heat, Percy cried, "Decide what?"

"If you want to stay with me here," his mother answered. "Or die out there."

The blistering heat made Percy nauseous. He leaned his head against his mother's frigid flesh, experiencing instant comfort. She stroked her fingers through his hair and whispered the words he longed to hear, a blurred hum in his ears. He slipped from consciousness: what started as a brilliant pinprick strengthened into a bright flash of light that expanded to engulf Percy, drawing him into oblivion. Percy clenched his eyes shut and screamed.

When Percy opened his eyes, the bright light burned into his retinas. His body jerked to the right, his hands tightly grasped around a bar that twisted in tune with his motion. Suddenly, the beam of light changed direction and passed him by; the growl of engines and squeal of brakes set Percy's heart fluttering. Beside him, his mother screeched, her hand dashing for the steering wheel…

Too late.

The front end of the car collided with an iron rail; the

boisterous thunder of crunching metal drowned out the sound of their screams as the vehicle flipped over the railing; for a moment, the Milky Way filled Percy's vision. He felt himself falling, defying gravity as it tugged at the Honda Accord. Landing with a gregarious boom, the roof caved in and a barrage of exploding glass shards clattered all around them. The impact set off the airbags, driver's side first, then the passenger side a split second after.

Upside down, the seatbelt cut into Percy's shoulder, and pain radiated from every nerve receptor in his body. "Mom," Percy said in a silent plea; his throat producing a dry, incoherent rasp. His fingers fumbled with his seatbelt, mustering the strength to depress the release mechanism. The buckle popped loose with a sharp snap, and Percy collapsed into a heap on the roof of the car, landing in a puddle of frigid, rushing water.

"Answer me, Mom." Percy found his voice.

Struggling, Percy pushed the inflated air bag aside, trying to reach his mother; the white fabric was stained with copious amounts of crimson blood. "Mom!" he repeated frantically as he fought against the air bag.

His mother's blood was staining his fingers.

The sound of clattering rocks tumbled down the embankment; Percy heard a man's voice calling out from outside, his voice rushing towards him. Footsteps splashed through water and the man's voice became clear. Realization struck Percy hard, a flood of memories flowing through his mind's eye.

The crunch of aluminum as he discarded his beer onto the driveway and stomped it flat. A moment of blackness, then his mother chasing after him as he staggered toward the car; her screaming at him to slow down; wrestling for control of the steering wheel; the way her flesh gave beneath his balled fist and the sound of her sobbing uncontrollably as he barked at her.

"Mom!" Percy cried out.

He yanked the air bag aside and retched at the sight of her skull caved in, the greyish bone beneath exposed. Fluids oozed from the gnarled gash, the river washing it away.

Percy filled his lungs and screamed for help. Outside, the stranger's panicked voice answered, begging him to stay still. He spoke on the phone with nine-one-one as he tried to pry the driver's side open. Percy begged the man to help his mother as the man ignored him. The world closed around him; blackness forcing itself over Percy.

"Send an ambulance.

"That's right, the Crooked Feeder bridge.

"One survivor…

"And one dead."

The pain became intolerable. Unable to fight it any longer, Percy slipped into oblivion.

Percy stared down at his stepfather, passed out in his recliner. Morgan Freeman's voice filled the silence. A peanut butter and jelly sandwich in one hand; and a kitchen knife lathered with strawberry jelly grasped in his balled fist. He took a bite of his sandwich, chewing on the thick layer of peanut butter, and tapped the knife off the seam of his jeans.

Percy finished the last of his lunch, gulped down a lump of bread, and picked up a half-empty beer can from the floor. He drained the rest in one swig, the bubbles frothing at the corner of his mouth and dribbling over his chin. With his fist, he crumpled the can and tossed it behind him on the floor.

Startled, Ben jumped upright in his chair, his eyes wide with bewilderment. "Jesus Christ, Percy," he stammered, still rousing from his drunken state. "You scared the shit out of me."

Percy continued to tap the stainless steel blade against his jeans.

"Where have you been?" Ben rubbed his forehead and squinted against the bright daylight filtering in through the living room window. "I've been worried sick about you."

Laughing, Percy shook his head and held the knife up to his face.

"What are you doing?"

"I did the dishes," Percy said, pointing the tip of the knife at Ben. "And I cleaned up the house for you, just as you asked."

Confused, Ben shook his head. "I don't know what's going on, Percy." His voice was wavering, fear quickening his words, jumbling them together. "I never asked you to do any of those things. But thanks."

"Someone around here has to keep up on the housework," he accused. "Ever since you drove Mom to kill herself."

Ben sighed deeply. "Why aren't you taking your medications, Percy?" He pointed to a cluster of amber bottles on the end table, all of them filled with brightly coloured pills and capsules. "We've talked about this. You're not well and I agree with the doctor. Maybe it's time we go back and see him."

"I'm not going into that place!" Percy screamed, thrusting the knife at Ben.

With nowhere else to go, Ben sank into the seat. He held up his trembling hand. "Let's be reasonable about this, Percy. You've suffered a tragic loss, and it's no wonder you're struggling to cope with it."

"Cope with it?" Percy guffawed. "By locking me up in that insane asylum?"

"It's a place to help you get better," Ben pleaded. "They only want to help you. I'm sorry, Percy, but I can't help you if you continue to refuse your medications."

Percy stomped a beer can flat. "Maybe I need to self medicate?

Ben stood up. Threatened, Percy took a step back and swung the knife in a violent arc. The blade sliced through Ben's throat with vicious ease. A clout of blood splattered over the floor before Ben could cover the savage gash with his hands. Blood gurgled in his throat as he tried to talk. He stumbled back into his chair — deep maroon blood oozed between his fingers and spilling over his white undershirt, soaking it to frail frame. It didn't take long for the gurgling sounds to cease; red stains smeared his pants and the cushion as his life blood pooled in his lap. His arms flailed over the sides, his head lolled to his shoulder, slumping deep into his chair.

Dazed, Percy wandered into the kitchen and laid the knife on the counter. Flecks of blood spattered the sink and wall, and dark red blood covered the stainless steel. The sight of it reminded him of his strawberry jam. He glanced over his shoulder at Ben, slumped over in his recliner, drunk again. Disgusted, Percy escaped through the back door and vowed to never come back again.

Hours later, as he strolled through the forest trail towards the tree house, the sound of police sirens blared in the distance.

With her fingers clasped, the figurine stared up at Angie from the cup of her hands. Her eyes wandered towards the ladder as she drew her lips against her teeth with a faint smile. "What is it supposed to be?" she asked as she rolled the glass ornament around, gazing at it with feigned interest.

"I got it for you," Percy said, his words tinged with anger and disappointment.

"You said that," Angie muttered. The light illuminated her strawberry blonde hair, giving her an ethereal aurora. She shifted uncomfortably back and forth on her feet, as if testing them to make sure they could still support her weight.

"If you don't like it," Percy snapped, snatching the glass figurine from her hand. "You can just say so." He stuffed the ornament in his back pocket, the glass pressed against his thigh and burned white hot.

"I think I should head back home," Angie said, shifting her weight onto her heels, bracing herself against Percy's advance. "My brother will be worried sick about me and if I'm late and get us in trouble…"

"Whatever," Percy interrupted, dismissing her with the wave of his hand. "Just leave, you fucking tease."

"Percy." Angie hesitated, inching towards the ladder and shaking her head. "That's not fair."

"You want to know what's not fair?" Percy asked,

taking a threatening step forward; Angie flinched at his advance. "My mother dying and no one caring. I spent months alone in the hospital. Except for Damien, no one visited me." Spittle flew from his mouth as he berated Angie. He took another staggering step forward, his breath rustling through Angie's hair.

Angie held up her hand, her fingers splayed wide open. "Now wait just a minute, Percy," she whimpered, back peddling towards the exit. In a fit of anxious panic, she misjudged the edge, the heel of her shoe plummeting through the open space. A blood-curdling scream tore through the forest, forcing a flutter of birds to dash into the night sky from a nearby tree. Somehow, Angie's fingertips grasped the wooden edge of the boards, saving her from falling straight down onto the root-tangled ground beneath. Terrified, her eyes grew wide and pleaded for help.

Infuriated with a sudden deep-seated rage, Percy's vision obscured by a blistering ball of white light. He shoved his palm against Angie's chest, enjoying the way it felt and regretted that it only lasted for a second; then her horrified scream faded as his vision slowly returned. When he adjusted, he stared at the sunset, Angie no longer blocking his view of the picturesque scenery.

"Angie," Percy called out, his tone flat and unnerving. An owl hooted somewhere near the lake, drawing his attention to the calm body of water. From up here, it reminded him of a black hole in space, the first signs of cabin lights around the lake bordering the dismal abyss. "You really should come up here and see this, Angie."

Percy stared down at her lifeless body, her right leg

twisted behind her backside, the shin bone exposed, torn through just below the knee. With her eyes wide open, she stared up at Percy, her expression still contorted in a state of disbelief. Fanned out around her, locks of her strawberry hair had stained scarlet. Percy noticed her left wrist snapped off, dangling from her limp arm at an awful angle. All around her, the earth bled.

Percy bust down the cottage door, startling Mary Lee and her boyfriend at the table as they played a game of strip poker. Mary Lee lunged for her shirt to cover herself up. The man tried to jump up to confront Percy, but his feet tangled in the folding chair, and he stumbled backwards, smashing the back of his head off the windowsill; he let out a defeated whimper as he slumped against the wall, a trail of blood traced his descent.

"I thought I told you to stay out of my cottage!" Percy bellowed.

"Jesus Christ, what are you screaming about?" the woman shouted as she recoiled from Percy. She rushed around the table and tended to her boyfriend; his head lolled heavily to one side as she grabbed his shoulders. "He's really hurt."

Turning her back to Percy, she begged her boyfriend to get to his feet. Percy made his way through the living room, heading straight past the couple and towards a door behind the fireplace. He threw the door open and stared into the wood closet, momentarily forgetting why. The woman's panicked voiced droned on in his head, a pain radiated from his temples. He grabbed his hair, pulling at it, begging for the sounds to stop.

"*The axe, Percy,*" his mother's voice spoke to him; gentle yet urgent.

Percy turned away from the closet, his hand resting on the handle, the thick wooden slab trying to sway open, tugging at him. The man ran his hand through his hair, grimacing in pain as he touched the nasty welt on the back of his hand, his palm bright red from the blood. With help from Mary Lee, the man stumbled to his feet, wobbling unsteadily on his legs. She ushered him over to the couch and did her best to guide him into the corner seat; he collapsed into the seat with a hard thump.

"Don't just stand there!" Mary Lee yelled at Percy. "Help me!" She got to her feet and glared at Percy; hatred fueled her aggression, giving her face a sharp edge. "This is all your fault, you know."

"You don't need to take that from her, Percy. Grab the axe and shut her up." His mother's voice was a sharp howl in his ear.

Percy could see the wooden handle jutting out from behind the door frame. Confused, Percy ran his fingers through the tangled mess of his hair and yanked at the roots. The room spun uncontrollably around him. His vision shifted Mary Lee's face into the veil of a horrible demon; red eyes peered at him from behind darkness, threatening him.

"Get up, Mike." Mary Lee tugged at Mike's collar. "I need to get you to the hospital."

"Don't let her leave or she'll get you in trouble. And we can't have that."

Corrupted by the sinister entity living within, Percy grabbed the axe; he enjoyed the way gravity tugged at the weight in his grasp as the heavy metal head of the axe stretched his shoulder muscles, begging him to use both hands.

"*That's a good boy, Percy,*" the voice hissed, no longer his mother's.

Percy held the axe across his chest, the blade raised towards the ceiling. Preoccupied with Mike, Mary Lee never noticed the blunt axe gripped tightly in his grasp. Or the wide-eyed, crazed expression of his face. Incensed by rage, Percy raised his arms high into the air, letting the head drop below to his backside; he shivered as the cold metal caressed his spine.

"*Kill them so we can be together.*"

Mike raised his hands to protect his face, mounting a pointless defense, and screamed as Percy brought the axe down. The blade sliced through his forearm, severing it with ease before continuing into Mike's stomach with a wet thunk, the axe head buried in the couch beneath; a gout of blood spattered onto the floor. With a gargled gasp, Mike stared down in disbelief as a coil of slimy gray intestine unfurled from his guts and slipped to the floor.

Terrified, Mary Lee raised her hands to cover a blood-curdling scream. In a state of disbelief, she staggered into the kitchen table, knocking the cards and poker chips to the floor with a crashing bang. A pained yelp escaped her throat as she grabbed at her hip. Placing one foot on the couch, Percy dislodged the axe head from the wooden frame and yanked the contents of Mike's stomach over the floor with a thick *plop*. When Percy turned towards Mary Lee, he found her racing towards the door.

"*Don't let her get away, Percy.*"

With all of his might, Percy heaved the axe. Guided

by unseen force with deadly accuracy, it spun across the room until the head buried into Mary Lee's back with a sickening *crack*. She fell unceremoniously into the door, her face smashing against the wood with a hard thump.

"*Good boy,*" the horrible voice cooed.

"I can't do this anymore," Percy said out loud to the voice in his head. "What is wrong with me?"

"*Too late now, Percy,*" the voice cackled. "*You can't take any of the things you've done back. They'll lock you away in an asylum for the rest of your life.*"

"I just want this to end," Percy answered, staring at Mary Lee's lifeless corpse slumped against the door. The wooden handle jutting towards Percy, begging him to retrieve it.

"*We can end your human suffering, child.*"

"You're not my mother, are you?" Percy asked, already knowing the answer. But he needed to the voice admit it.

A chorus of voices answered Percy in a disturbing harmonic symphony. "*Your mother held out against our will until the day she abandoned you. She thought she could protect you from us. But she didn't realize you need us.*"

"Who are you?" Percy growled.

"*The ancestors of your past and future. And we will set you free from your human body and release you from your suffering.*"

"Just tell me what to do."

"*Burn away your sins.*"

Percy stared at the wooden fireplace with cruel intentions.

XVII. Life or Death

"Why won't you help me, Mom?" Percy begged as the acidic smoke stung his eyes and burned his lungs. "I don't want to go with them anymore."

A tear tracked down her cheek as she shook her head; black strands of hair fell over her face, obscuring a sad, defeated expression. "It's too late." she whispered. She pulled him close, embracing him with her cool touch. "What's done is done."

"Why did you lead me into this forsaken cottage?" Percy asked, his voice flared with anger.

"Understand that it was never my voice inside your head," his mother said as the fire consumed the surrounding walls. A blistering heat filled the room, beads of sweat poured from Percy's forehead. "They tricked you, and now it's too late for you to escape them."

"Who are they and why did they wait for me?"

"The cursed souls of your ancestors who have been waiting for an opportunity to enter our world."

"Are you telling me the Shaman was my grandfather?"

Percy's mother tilted her head back and cackled. "I said your ancestors, Percy. You are part of something mystical, from beyond this world. Since you were born, you've known you were different. Our race can be traced back to the days of the building of Stonehenge. The curse that plagues us has travelled many galaxies and has existed for centuries, placed upon us by Merlin himself to stop us from taking back what rightfully belongs to us."

"What are you telling me? That I'm an alien from another world?"

"We are from another time and place, beyond this world. Our people have been waiting eons for you, our resurrected conqueror."

"And what do they want with me?" Percy asked, afraid to hear the answer. His clothes clung to his body, fixed in place by layers of sweat.

"You will be their vessel in this world," she spoke with no emotion, her voice flat.

Percy turned towards his mother, hurt by the sight of her blank expression. "Mom, you're scaring me. Please, I want to go with you." A shrill cackle thundered from the walls, booming around him. "What will happen to me when you leave me by myself?"

"Percy, you will never need to be afraid again," his mother said as she stood up. The emerald of her eyes replaced by a diseased, vile green, her flesh turned rotten and black. "They will guide you to your destiny and strengthen your resolve." With no warning, the flames engulfed his mother.

The flames fed on Percy. He smelled the sick aroma of burning flesh. Blisters formed all over his body, swelling into translucent bubbles before bursting in a spray of yellow puss. His skin blackened and peeled back, revealing the scorched flesh beneath; blackened blood coursed through the veins that snaked through his body.

"What do they want from me?" Percy screamed, calling out for his mother.

"*Vengeance,*" the cruel voice answered in his mother's place.

Agony fled from Percy's body as the pain was replaced by euphoric bliss as a second skin fused over his charred remains. Engulfed in flames, a profound energy coursed through his veins, feeding his muscles with vigorous strength.

"*And you will provide it for us.*"

XVIII. S.P.E.A.R

With a vacant expression, Damien stared out of the pane glass window at the garden; his elbows leaned against the windowsill, while his chin was propped up by his cupped hands. Organized in rows, colourful beds of flowers bordered the stone pathway. The boisterous racket of a lawnmower blared just out of sight as the caretakers attended to the lawn with meticulous attention to detail. They trimmed the hedges into one seamless rectangle in order to conceal the depressing wrought iron bars contained within.

Overhead, the sky was a light denim, the sun a blazing ball of yellow fury scorching the grass, forcing the sprinklers to work overtime. A pleasant breeze pushed a cluster of clouds across the horizon, ushering them away from the sun. Gaggling on the lawn, a murder of crows probed for worms buried within the luscious grass; the festering black feathers littered the grounds.

"Damien Colbourne." a throaty voice snapped the silence, bringing Damien back to reality.

Damien turned his attention towards the man, detecting a lingering bouquet of tobacco and vanilla from the stranger. His well-trimmed beard gleamed with oil in the harsh florescent light. He pulled the desk chair out and hauled it beside the bed, the legs scraping across the floor; the sound made Damien cringe. A badge dangled from a lanyard draped around his neck, the gold border shining brightly, obscuring the markings as the golden glare forced Damien to squint his eyes shut. Before he sat down, the man rummaged through his jacket pocket and hauled out a recording device, placing it on the table; a burst of static hissed through the speakers, then faded away. The man rested a clipboard across his lap, andhe tapped a pen off the metal clip holding the sheets in place.

"I'm Detective Anderson," he started, then examined the recording device before continuing. "Your file floated across my desk the other day and I've asked the staff doctors at this institution permission to speak with you today. Do you mind if we discuss the events that occurred at Deadman's Lake here today — without your lawyer?"

"Whatever," Damien grumbled, raising his hand above his head and flicking it with a dismissive wave.

The detective studied Damien's face and shook his head. "Damien—" he paused. "Do you mind if I call you by your first name?"

"Go ahead," Damien answered with a shrug of his shoulders.

Anderson smiled and nodded his head. "Before we begin, how have you been sleeping?"

"Not bad," Damien lied. He instantly recognized the expression on the detective's face: that he wasn't fooled by Damien's feeble attempt.

Thumbing through the pages on the clipboard, Anderson tapped the paper with his index finger when he found the right page. "Are you still having the night terrors?"

"No."

Anderson exhaled deeply. "Why are you lying to me, young man?"

"I've already told them my story," Damien snapped. He thrust an accusing finger at the clipboard. "You've read through it all. Can we get this over with? I'm sick to my stomach talking about Percy Benoit."

"Listen, Damien," Anderson said. He lowers his voice two octaves and jabbed the clipboard with the tip of his pen: "I'm here to do my job and we need your help to find Percy. As I'm sure you're aware, he's committed some serious crimes and we aren't buying any of this bull." Anderson banged the clipboard off the arm of the metal chair. "Just start from the beginning."

Damien stared at the detective, his hazel eyes teeming with disgust, his lips pressed against his teeth in a false smile. "All my problems started the week after he crashed his car."

Anderson's eyes darted back and forth across the page, studying his notes and trying to keep the stories straight. He mumbled something inaudible under his breath, turned the page and thumbed through it. "Can you elaborate?" His voice was firm, demanding.

"Percy refused to accept that he killed his mother. He drank himself into oblivion and something horrendous happened to him in the abyss." Damien hesitated. "Because of the abuse."

"Yes, we've pulled out all the medical reports," Anderson said, flipping to the last pages on his clipboard. "Found several complaints of the stepfather's abuse. But they confirmed that all of Percy's wounds were self in-flicted."

"He made Ben out to be such a monster." Damien sighed and shook his head. "Worst part is that we be-lieved him. Ben could be a real asshole, drunk off his ass most days. It all made sense."

"No one's here to judge you," Anderson grunted. "Go on. And you can skip to the night of Angie's disappear-ance. We have collaborating stories to confirm your sto-ries from the night of the bonfire at Deadman's Lake."

"After telling me an elaborate tale about Ben and his mother, Percy left my house to meet with Angie in the tree house." Damien paused, trying to remember why they were meeting. "If I remember correctly, he wanted to give her something he found. When I visited him later that night, he seemed agitated."

"Did he give you a reason why?"

"He said something about the people that bought the old cottage were out to get him." Damien stopped and stared at Anderson as he thumbed through his paper-work. "Could you stop doing that? It's really annoying."

Anderson held up a finger, not bothering to take his eyes off his paperwork. "They list the cabin under Ben Benoit's name. No new owners."

"I'm just telling you what Percy said. If you don't want me to…"

Anderson grunted, "When did you last see Angie?"

Rendered silent, Damien stared wide-eyed at the de-tective, surprised by the question.

Anderson pulled a sheet of paper from the clipboard and passed it to Damien. "We pulled her cell phone record. Seems like you texted her phone after she left the treehouse. Were you jealous of Percy's relationship with Angie?"

"No," Damien snapped, his voice seething with rage; he shook uncontrollably. "Yeah, I texted her that night." He stared down at the recorded conversation, the paper wavering in his shaky hands. The paper fell from his hand and floated to the floor, landing on its edge with a sharp retort.

"You texted her phone," Anderson said, holding up his finger.

"What?" Damien asked, growing annoyed.

"Percy had her phone," he answered, ignoring Damien's tone. "He must have been texting you from it. I think he used it to draw you and her brother out to the cottage."

"Why would you think that?"

Not bothering to acknowledge Damien's question, Anderson continued. "What time did you meet with Percy?" Anderson pressed the question.

"I don't recall," Damien answered, avoiding Anderson's prying gaze.

Anderson leaned forward, the chair squeaking beneath him with coffee heavy on his breath. "Convenient," he said, his voice laden with sarcasm; he tapped his pen against the clipboard and glanced out the window. "You didn't mention any of this before. Now, why is that, Damien?" Anderson refused to let it go. With a shit-eating smile plastered across his face, he glared at Damien.

"Because," Damien sighed. "None of this is relevant to what happened that night."

"Tell me about the lights."

"How—?" Damien asked, astonished.

Anderson didn't meet his gaze, his eyes glued to his paperwork, darting across the pages, absorbing the details of Damien's medical diagnosis.

Damien felt his heart thrash against his ribcage. "We all witnessed the lights in the cottage that night." Damien lowered his head into his outstretched palms. "I can still see them in my head... Indescribable horrors. Every time I close my eyes, I see them." Damien shuddered, a tear welling in the corner of his eye.

Anderson leaned forward, his breath overpowering. "That's the part of the story nobody believes. But despite what people might think or say, I'm here because I may be one of the few people in the world that know you're telling the truth. Can you describe them to me?"

"S-strange lights that d-danced in the sky," Damien stuttered. "I've never seen nothing like it before."

"Do you think aliens abducted your friends?"

"No, that's not what I think," Damien hisses. "Can you understand the reason why I stopped telling the truth?" Damien got to his feet with his hands curled into fists by his side.

Anderson leaned back in his chair and motioned for Damien to take a seat. "How did her brother end up out there with you?"

"He went to the cottage searching for his sister," Damien answered as he took a seat on the edge of his bed; the springs sang as he sat down. He felt cornered by the interrogation, pushed towards his already diminished brink of sanity.

"Do you know why he went out there looking for her?" Anderson's pen scribbled across the margin of a page, then hovered, waiting for Damien's response.

"Percy told him that the owners of the cottage abducted her," Damien said, shaking his head. "That they were holding her hostage in the attic. But we didn't know any better." Overwhelmed, he buried his face in his hands, fighting back the flood of emotions threatening to burst forth.

"Why didn't you call the cops?"

Damien glared at Anderson in astonishment. "Because no one would accept the stories Percy fabricated. I don't understand how, but he fooled us into trusting his stories."

Anderson reached out and laid his hand on Damien's shoulder, squeezing gently. The gentle interaction pushed him over the edge, breaking the pent-up dam of emotions that had been building up. "Percy took them away!" Damien cried, wiping the tears away with the back of his sleeve.

Anderson took out a folded handkerchief from his inside pocket and handed it over to Damien. "Where did he take them?"

"Deep into the woods," Damien answered, wiping the tears away as they track down his face in rivers.

"Are they dead?" Anderson's voice fell flat, hopeless.

After an agonizing pause, Damien whispered, "Yes. But you've already discovered that, didn't you?"

"I just need to know if I can trust you," Anderson said, reaching for the recording device. He turned it off. The digital tape warbled static, then grew dead silent. "This stays between you and me. Can you handle that?"

"Nobody believes a word I say." Damien spat the words out with venomous anger. "Not even my own parents."

Anderson nodded his head. "They found Ben Benoit slumped in his recliner, his neck open from ear to ear. We discovered the remains of Angie at the base of that damn treehouse. And we found the other bodies in a shallow grave along the beach. The police still don't have the victim's identity."

"How do you have that before the police?"

"The toxicology reports came back with a, how would you put it, unusual substance they found… lodged into the bones." Anderson paused, deep in thought. "Our office gets notified when anything out of the ordinary gets entered into any police system. It blocks the data from being passed on to the authorities until we can analyze the data ourselves."

"Who do you work for?"

"I work for a government agency called SPEAR." Anderson pulled his wallet out of his pocket and showed Damien his real ID. "Agent Patrick Anderson," he said, extending his hand. "We investigate the cases that everyone else refuses to consider pursuing. Our scope extends far beyond the realm of possibilities." Anderson glanced over his shoulder at the door before showing Damien a photograph at the back.

Bile raced up Damien's throat, burning the flesh of his esophagus. He turned away from the horrendous photograph and heaved. A splatter of vomit splashed off the floor. "What is that?" Damien gasped.

"That's a picture of Stan's ribcage. A hunter discovered his body deep in the forest, about a mile south of the highway. There are bite marks all over the bones. Our coroner confirmed the imprints left behind are a match to Percy Benoit's dental records. But with a tremendous amount of force, not capable of being made by the human jaw. Especially not by a troubled teen." He flipped to another picture. "Do you recognize these two people?"

"We ran into those people at the cottage the morning everything happened."

"You mean you and Percy?"

"Yes." Damien stared at their pictures. "Her name is Mary Lee. I didn't catch his name."

"What were they doing there?"

"They wanted to break into the cottage. At first, Percy helped them out. But once they were inside, he lost his mind and screamed at them. Kicked them out, screaming at them to never come back," Damien said, frowning. "They said they'd be back later that night. Percy warned them never to come back."

"Did he tell them that the cottage belonged to him?" Anderson's pen scribbled across the back of the photograph.

Damien shook his head. "I never even realized that his family owned it. Percy never talked about it before — they never talked about staying there before."

"After the accident, I assume he visited the cottage a lot more to spend time with his mother. And I recognize this sounds crazy, but I believe a malevolent spirit infected Percy's soul. I'm sure if a doctor tried to diagnose him, they'd label him as a paranoid schizophrenic."

"What are you saying?"

"SPEAR needs to know where Percy Benoit is Damien," Anderson said with a sense of urgency rushing his words. "And I appreciate you understand why."

"I… I can't explain it." Damien broke into tears again and took a few seconds before gasping, "But I think that he's coming for me."

Anderson nodded his head in agreement. "In your nightmares…" he hesitated, mulling for the right phrase. "I understand why you would consider something like that. But this is far worse. Percy isn't like you or me. He's not human. Not anymore. I need your help to stop him from harming anyone else."

"I… Ha. Afraid I can't help you," Damien sobbed, gasping out a wet laugh that wasn't a laugh at all. "I'm terrified of Percy. He's haunted me ever since I ran into him that night in the forest. The only peace I've gotten has come inside of these walls. Somehow, this place keeps me safe.

"And I'm not going back to Crooked Creek. Percy killed those people and he tried to kill me. If he can't get me in here, his reign of terror is over."

Anderson lowered his head and sighed. "So, nobody has told you about the other kids in your class?"

Damien shook his head. "How many?"

"Three of them over the last two months. I believe that's about the time you got locked away in here."

Damien nodded his head in agreement.

"Why didn't he kill you that night?"

"I-I can't…" Damien stammered. "I don't understand."

"You're his best friend and somehow he restrained himself from killing you. Haunting you may have kept him occupied. But now that you're out of his reach, he's killing again." Anderson placed his hands over Damien's and said, "You can help me."

"How?"

"Percy will come for you," Anderson said, locking his gaze on Damien's. "And when he does, it's better that we're there with you. Wouldn't you agree?"

Damien stared up at the detective and simply nodded his head.

Afterword

There is one reason I wrote this book: I wanted to write something that my wife would enjoy. She's a big fan of thrillers, and I decided I should at least attempt to write something just for her. While it is riddled with references to my favorite author, and in the end, veers off course into something you'd expect to see from me, it's my best attempt at a true thriller. So, I hope that this novel finds a special place on your bookshelf with all your favourites. I hope that you, the reader, will enjoy it as well.

I want to thank Matthew LeDrew for inviting me to his wonderful writing class. I did my best to take all the things you taught me about the Harmon Circle while also using everything else I learned in your course. It made me a better writer and I'm eternally grateful. I also want to give a shout out to all the supportive members who attended the class with me and helped me turn this novel into something better.

I want to thank all my family and friends for being supportive and always bragging about my novels to your friends and family. An extra special thanks goes out to Dana and Rick, who are patient enough to sit with me while I write and allow me to spend time typing away at the computer. Another extra special thanks to my editor, Erin Vance, for agreeing to edit my books even after all the

nightmares (literal and literary) I've caused you. And, of course, another special thanks to Ellen Curtis for the amazing cover. It captures the tone of this book perfectly and I couldn't be prouder to have it represent my work.

Last but certainly not least, I want to thank Jon Dobbin and Brad Dunne. You guys inspire me to be a better writer and your feedback and encouragement keep me moving forward.

Did you enjoy the work of Paul Carberry?
Read his other short fiction in Engen's bestselling anthologies, including *Terror Nova*, *Chillers from the Rock*, *Fantasy from the Rock*, *Flights from the Rock* and *From the Rock Stars*.

The From the Rock series features short stories written by a diverse mix of the best authors in Canada, including award-winning veterans of their craft, and brand new talent.

Also featuring the work of Ali House (*The Segment Delta Archives*), Matthew LeDrew (*Coral Beach Casefiles*, *The Xander Drew series*), Jon Dobbin (*The Starving*), and more!

These collections showcases the talent, imagination, and prestige that Canada has to offer. From stories of censorship gone awry to sentient buses, global warming to corporate-branded culture, these collections have it all!

ABOUT THE AUTHOR

Paul Carberry is a huge proponent of the horror genre and its place in literature. He has two children, daughter Dana and son Rick, with his wife Leah.

Paul has published six novels with Engen Books: the four-novel *Zombies on the Rock* series, *Carcharodon*, and *The Cottage Across the Lake*. He has also had numerous short stories featured in publication in anthologies such as *From the Rock* and *Terror Nova*, including The Light of Cabot Tower, Into the Forest, and Halloween Mummers.

His seventh novel, *The Last Dragon*, will be released in 2022.